POISON

So that was it. Aunt Lollie's bonbons, the weakness, the cramps. But why hadn't it killed her? Because Aunt Mellie hadn't wanted it to, only doled it out with a sparse hand. She'd merely wanted to see her sister in trouble, to make her suffer. This must have been going on for years.

No wonder they didn't want me, hadn't willingly sent for me! Two sisters practicing their nefarious rites upon each other—what was the reason for all of it? Aunt Lollie hinted at trouble back in England.

Or was there something more to it? I had begun to suspect something deeper and far more sinister which led them to this end . . .

THE SECRETS OF MONTROTH HOUSE

MURIEL NEWSOME

DIAMOND BOOKS, NEW YORK

THE SECRETS OF MONTROTH HOUSE

A Diamond Book / published by arrangement with
the author

PRINTING HISTORY
Diamond edition / March 1992

ISBN: 1-55773-678-2

THE SECRETS OF MONTROTH HOUSE

Prologue

EVERY TIME I HEAR THUNDER roar across a leaden sky or drum like a thousand demons around the rim of the world, I remember Montroth.

It did not frighten me then, the storm that was my introduction to a new land, for, England-born, I was no stranger to rain. But it seems to me, looking back after more than six years, that even the weather was trying to warn me against entering Montroth that first time. The memories of the brooding mansion hidden away so strangely in the Canadian wilderness remain to haunt me still. Jagged lightning and drumming rain on a roof pull me back, against my will, to that night I first set eyes upon what was to be my home for those fateful months and plunge me into such terrible danger. Those who perished there, the two tiny great-aunts who were my last living relatives, my worry and my despair, cannot come back, nor, much as I loved them, would I will it so.

The one bright spot during that time was the stranger I met and, yes, loved, from that first stormy night of my arrival.

But I get ahead of my story. . . .

~ 1 ~

April 1895

"LORENE KILMER?"

A tug on my elbow whirled me around. "Aunt Mellie? Oh, I am so glad to see you!" My first impression was an overwhelming odor of mothballs mingled with wet wool, and I resisted the impulse to reach out and put my arms around the diminutive woman. "I was beginning to wonder—did you have trouble?"

Age had touched her lightly, except that she seemed even smaller than I remembered. How old was she, around sixty? No, I thought, in her mid-seventies, Aunt Lollie two years younger. Sharp blue eyes in a pink cherub face belied the signs of aging in her—thin lips tucked purse-tight and her feathery white hair squashed beneath a soggy felt hat. She wore black gloves, a long raincoat over her old woolen jacket, and carried an enormous knitted handbag.

For a moment there was silence as she coolly took my measure, and I began to feel uncomfortable beneath the piercing stare. She appeared to be disappointed, or regretful, or both. Then she frowned. "Trouble? Humph. It is a trip I would not undertake by choice."

"It's far, then. I hope you—"

She cut me off. "We were mired coming in, I daresay we shall become mired going back. A wonder the bridges are not entirely washed out."

If I had expected her to embrace me or otherwise show warmth toward a grandniece she hadn't seen for sixteen years, I would have been disappointed. Instead she said in a sharp, disbelieving tone, "I don't recall your age. How old are you—twenty?"

"Twenty-five." I looked around. "I take it Aunt Lollie didn't come. Is she well?"

"No. However, she has only a slight indisposition which will clear up shortly. How was the voyage?"

"The ocean was rough," I admitted, "and I thought I would never see land again. I am so very glad to be here at last."

"All right. If you are ready, let us get on with it. We haven't all day."

She was admirably capable, and between the two of us we found someone to help with the bags. I had already cleared customs, and once outside, she led the way to a waiting carriage, trotting ahead beside the boy with the luggage.

It was still early morning but was heavily overcast with gathered storm clouds and it seemed to me, coming from the warmth of indoors, that the drops were more snow than rain. Head down, I didn't see the figure looming directly in my path and ploughed full tilt into it.

"Oh, I beg your pardon!" My eyes traveled up and up—the man was over six feet and I am short—to a dark, annoyed face. It was then I saw I'd knocked the traveling bag out of his hand and that it had fallen and sprung open, strewing an array of men's socks, shirts and personal belongings. "I *am* sorry," I cried, aghast, scooping up a small bar of soap folded in a flannel case and handing it to him, "here—let me help."

"Thank you, but no. I appreciate the offer, but I can manage." His voice was deep, compelling, with an American accent. An outdoorsman, I thought, almost swarthy with strong, rugged features and gray eyes that appraised me as frankly as I was covertly appraising him. I knew what

I looked like and it wasn't my best; wrinkled from travel and with all the carefully coaxed-in curl of my blonde hair plastered to my cheeks from the wet.

He was grinning, no longer annoyed. "Barely a hundred pounds, isn't it? Your aim is outstanding, I couldn't have executed a better blocking maneuver myself. I'd no idea you were going to turn to the left."

"There was a puddle." I defended myself feebly as I watched him stow a dripping sock. "It was careless of me and all my fault. I wasn't looking where I was going."

"No, you weren't," he agreed cheerfully. The bag snapped shut and he got to his feet, still eyeing me. "If I were a famous ambassador carrying secret papers I wouldn't stand a chance with you around. But as you know, there is nothing in here that won't bear inspection or that won't dry out, so no harm done." He glanced back toward the building then moved into step beside me. "The elements aren't cooperating too well, but with a late spring, it's what we can expect in this part of the country. And rain does clear the air."

"You sound as if you liked it here. You're Canadian?" I knew I was being bold in speaking freely. I had never done so before and couldn't think why I was doing so now.

"No," he said, "but I work out of British Columbia occasionally. As an independent, I travel around to evaluate stands of timber for logging operations. My name is Landrau—Stephen Landrau." He put out his hand and, under the same compulsion, I placed mine in it.

"Lorene Kilmer, and I'm sorry I upset your things. I mean that."

"I can see you do. You have the sunniest smile."

"And the wettest feet." I drew my hand away regretfully. "Light walking shoes are hardly suitable for this kind of weather." I looked down at them ruefully. "I should have worn waders."

"A sense of humor too. I like that. Are you in British Columbia to stay or to visit?"

"To stay."

"Then maybe we'll meet again."

"There is not much chance of that, because I won't be living in town." I stole a glance at this Stephen Landrau; he caught me looking, and grinned. I wondered if my own smile wasn't a trifle uncertain. Even though we'd only exchanged a few words, I was afraid I wouldn't be seeing Stephen Landrau again either.

"Since you're a newcomer, can I welcome you? At the risk of being forward, I'd like to offer a cup of hot coffee, or tea, only I gather that's out of the question anyway, since we seem to be going the wrong direction and in quite a hurry." He stopped. "By the way, where are we going?"

I'd halted too. I felt guilty. "I'm supposed to be following my aunt. She went ahead with the luggage." I grasped the strap of my reticule more firmly and looked around. Aunt Mellie was already out of sight. Which way she'd gone, I didn't know. The best thing, I decided, was to wait where I was.

"Did she come out this direction?"

"I thought so, but I don't see her. She can't be far." Somehow it was so easy to talk to him. "My great-aunt. She's one of two. I've only just arrived from England, and Aunt Mellie came to meet me."

"Great-aunts." He shook his head. "I should have guessed. Doesn't every English girl have one or more, dowagers with cameo brooches on lace collars at their necks? They all carry canes and wear gold ornaments pinned to their flat bosoms."

I had a sudden flash of memory and laughed, I couldn't help it. He was more right than he knew. "Millicent and Letitia," I said. "Aunt Lollie, practical as a butterfly, has always been my champion. Aunt Mellie is made of sterner stuff, orderly and a bit grim. Maybe not grim, but stern." And frightening, I could have added. It was Aunt Mellie who, with an iron hand, had managed her own and her sister's affairs for as long as I could remember. At five, I had stood terribly in awe of her; at nine, when they were virtually recluses, I had accepted my duty visits with resignation and not a little fear.

"I gather it's some time since you've seen either of them. Did you recognize the one who came to meet you?"

"Oh yes. Of course. Actually, she'd changed very little." I'd had a likeness of them last year. Aunt Lollie's image was badly blurred, but there was no mistaking stiff-jawed little Aunt Mellie.

"I'd like to look you up," Stephen Landrau said. His gaze was steady and held my own, and I felt a heady warmth course through me. "Would you mind?"

I had expected it and wasn't surprised. He was completely serious and so was I. But how could I direct anyone to my new home when I didn't know where it was myself, other than that my letters to my great-aunts were addressed to, and theirs posted from, Moose Station, British Columbia. "You would never find the place," I heard myself say, "and that's the only answer I can give. Even I don't know where it is—I've been told it's only a blank spot on the map."

"There are those in the province." Rain ran down his collar and dripped off. My hat was soaked, and I could feel fingers of rain on my face, but I didn't care. "Look, you can't just walk away like this," he said. "Fade into the wilderness and—at least let me wait with you until she comes."

"No, that is not necessary," I said. "I saw you looking back, I know you have business elsewhere. You were on your way somewhere when we met. I'll be fine. Really." My throat felt tight.

"Then if you're sure—"

He held out his hand again, touched mine, and turned. I watched him stride away, and felt suddenly at a loss, a ship in a lonely sea. I liked his assurance, the easy way he carried himself, the way we laughed together. Most of all, I liked his grin, frank and appreciative of what he saw. It had been such a wonderful interlude, but all too brief. Why hadn't I at least told him he could come? He might have been able to find the place.

I blinked the mist from my eyes then moved swiftly to meet the taut little figure advancing toward me.

"Where had you gone? I thought you were right behind me. You should have made an effort to keep up. The carriage was late. Most inefficient! Who was that you were talking to?"

"Just—" I hesitated, "someone I bumped into. I knocked his bag out of his hand and his belongings fell all over the ground." Sharp eyes, I thought, she'd never miss a thing.

"Did you know him? No? Then you must take care. Hasn't anyone told you not to speak to strangers? Well, do hurry, we're wasting time."

I climbed into the carriage, and we were off, whisking through streets whose names I could not have remembered if I had tried. Nor were my efforts at conversation rewarded, but Aunt Mellie's crisp yes, no, and I don't know failed to dampen my spirits. It would take more than a bristly little old lady to do that. And I loved her, I truly did. It was just that I was grown up now and glad to find myself past the point of intimidation. But somewhere there was a key to unlock her stony little heart, and I vowed I'd find it.

We left the carriage at a railway station. I asked if the train we boarded would take us all the way home, and was answered with a brief, "No. Do not be impatient."

I tried to obey and to ignore my stomach's rumbling. It was well past noon. Either there was no dining car on the line or she chose to ignore the fact.

It was a journey through incredible scenery. The train plunged into deep gorges and labored across narrow trestles hundreds of feet above boiling white rivers. The light was abruptly dimmed by dank rock walls dripping with green fungus and bracken. Our fragile steel path penetrating ranks of trees whose tops were lost in fog. The country, young, vigorous, and so unlike the placid streams and smooth worn hills I was accustomed to, greatly appealed to me. It was like leaving one world and going into another, and if it hadn't been for the conviction that in some strange fashion

I was burning my bridges, I could have relaxed and enjoyed the experience.

I hadn't counted on being so isolated. I could have remained in England to sidestep George and a union I didn't desire. But my father would have wanted me with my great-aunts after he was gone, not only for my own sake, but to be with them in their declining years.

I'd sent word of his passing to them and shortly received a terse reply. Come. There was plenty for me to do. Montroth's library was in a terrible state, and I was to put it in order for eventual sale. Nothing was said about their looking forward to seeing me, but I'd hardly expected it, so the omission didn't bother me too much. I was only glad to have the situation on a firm basis from the start. It was an opportunity to get away, renew acquaintance with two aged aunts, and happily to return to my first love—working with books. In the meantime, I was to remember that if she hadn't wanted me to come she wouldn't have asked.

Stiffly upright, Aunt Mellie took no note of scenery or route, and I had the notion that she had just one urge— to reach her home. I felt a rush of warmth for the little old lady at my side for having come all this way only to about-face and travel back again. She would have napped on the train and perhaps in the carriage as well, but it was still too much for one of her years. I knew that to voice my concern would be an insult, so I said, "It's beautiful—very different, but don't you get lonely, so far out?"

"What for?" she snorted. "We have Montroth and things exactly the way we want them."

"But you do have visitors, don't you?"

"Once in a while, of course. Everyone has visitors. We realize there is an outside world, but we want nothing to do with it. We left it once and will not return."

I wanted to ask why, but that would be overstepping my bounds too. After all, I supposed they could live where they chose. The aunts were of old and sol-id family, with sufficient means to gratify their every whim, even to constructing their home in the back end of nowhere.

Why these two had decided to relocate so far from their native land I didn't know, and they kept their own counsel. As representative for a book-binding firm, my father traveled a great deal. Since my mother died when I was born, I traveled with my father when I grew old enough, so we were out of the country at the time of the aunts' move. As to reasons for that move, I confessed I didn't know. Perhaps, I thought, the last of the Montroths had made up their minds to be completely different.

I glanced sidewise at my companion. "Have you had any visitors recently?"

Aunt Mellie gave me a sharp look. "Not recently, no. Some time ago there was a young man, Werner Venson, who stopped by. Unfortunately he was able to remain with us only a few days."

Venson. Where had I heard that name before? It escaped me.

"What was he doing there? Did he come especially to visit?"

"No," she snapped, "he was on his way to the coast and I believe he became lost, though he did not say so. Employed by a dredging concern, whatever that is."

A dredging concern. Poor Mr. Venson could well have become lost, was my inner verdict as I stared up the trunks of those forest giants we passed. Stephen Landrau would never find me, even if he was of a mind to come as he had said.

We left the train at dusk, in the same vicious downpour. The hills crouched on either side of the tracks were nearly obliterated by rain; the rough plank platform was almost awash, rain roping off the eaves of the station.

"Is this it?" I asked and looked around amazed, but Aunt shook her head.

"Not yet." Though the building was locked, the office plainly deserted with but one oil lamp burning behind the

wicket, Aunt Mellie was unruffled. We were the only pas-
sengers to disembark, and the cheery red glow of the light
on the last car was swallowed up immediately in the gloom.
Yet hadn't I the impression of a figure—a large figure
the size and build of Stephen Landrau—leaving the train
farther forward, fading at once into the dusk? Something
about the cut of the shoulders—I couldn't be sure. It was a
brief glimpse only, and I told myself I must be mistaken.

"We will wait," Aunt Mellie stated firmly, and wait we
did, pushed close to the building's side to keep out of
the wet.

A coach presently arrived to pick us up—huge and box-
like and pulled by a single dray horse, but a coach nonethe-
less, and patently out of place in all this heaving wilderness.
As the vehicle pulled to a halt, it skidded heavily sidewise
into a rut, and with much splashing and backing the driver
extricated it from the ooze and up to higher ground. By the
time the door opened, I'd laid hands on some of the bags
myself, but it was a slippery business, struggling with a case
in either hand and tripping over my skirts in an attempt to
keep my feet.

"Jason," panted Aunt Mellie, gesturing wildly as we
neared the coach, "however did you manage to get yourself
bogged in such a fashion? Up against the station wall there
are the rest of the bags—step lively, now! And hurry"—she
looked to me—"we are getting most dreadfully wet!"

I tried to conceal my shock as Jason moved from behind
the vehicle to confront us. Very little taller than Aunt
Mellie, he was old, his hunchbacked figure enveloped in
oilskins to his knees. He was hatless, his head bearing
a great bush of grizzled hair which dripped rain steadily
into his open collar. He spoke not a word, and I realized,
again with shock, that he was mute. With absolute, doglike
devotion, he glowed at Aunt Mellie, his smile gentle, that
of a child. He looked at me with curiosity which was
also that of a child—then bewilderment and something
else which might have been horror. Then he bobbed his

head, acknowledging me; the bags stowed in the boot, he held the door and closed it after us with an old-fashioned, courtly grace.

"Don't be alarmed," Aunt Mellie reassured me, "Jason is a fine driver, he has been doing this for years. An accident—remind me to tell you about it sometime."

She tucked herself firmly into her corner, her little face turned to me and asked if I nursed. I was startled. A simple illness, but anything more serious—I didn't know.

"Is there someone sick at the house?"

"Not necessarily. A handy skill to have about should there be the need."

"But you said—Aunt Lollie isn't—"

"She is a fool!" Aunt Mellie gritted out between clenched teeth. "At the moment Letitia is very much alive. She will be at table tonight, provided she has not stuffed herself with those dreadful chocolates she dotes on, and made herself ill again. She has done so before, you know. I find my sister extremely trying at times."

The assertion forbade comment, so I made none. Instead, I turned the conversation to my duties. Yes, there would be cataloguing in plenty. The library was in terrible shape. I was to take my time and do a good job. Aunt Lollie was a stupid romantic, but she, Aunt Mellie, preferred more robust literature.

"Naturally you enjoy reading, Lorene."

"Call me Lori. Everybody does."

"I shall call you Lorene. That is your name."

"Very well." I sighed. There were bound to be shoals ahead. Living in the same house with two old ladies, one of whom struck sparks, might not be as easy as I'd thought.

"Are you hungry?"

"Very much so," I admitted. "I've had no lunch, only breakfast, and that was a long time ago." I didn't mention my prodigious appetite.

"Try these." She reached in the bag and brought out several paper-wrapped green squares of something which looked like solidified wax, but I was certain was not.

"Mints," she offered briefly. "Homemade. My—Mrs. Lupti, Hessit, that is, makes them for me. Good for dyspepsia."

"You have dyspepsia?" I asked, thinking that possibly the reason for the irritability.

"No I do not and will you stop nattering at me? I never saw such a girl!"

I felt my hackles rise and smoothed them down with an effort.

Nearing the estate, Aunt Mellie eagerly pointed out landmarks. Up ahead was the entrance to the drive; there, to the south, the valley. Montroth mansion stood upon a lovely flat area. Well, it wasn't a mansion actually, Aunt Mellie explained, they only called it that. It was simply a big house, rambling and quite drafty in winter; however, they did have fireplaces, and Jason kept them well supplied with wood.

Could I see toward the east, the break in the trees? she asked. That was the entrance to the driveway. I looked, and in the gloom could see nothing at all save the narrow rutted road before us, sheeted with rain, and the thrashing branches of the evergreens on either side.

Slowly we entered the drive itself, which was unkempt and forbidding, a long black tunnel leading into some unknown sepulcher. Here and there beside it, where the evergreens had fallen away, I glimpsed dense entanglements of brush and some kind of native tree whose branches, still naked this late April, interwove in sinuous embrace. Nearer the road, to the right, rose an embankment six feet or so in height, which appeared threatened by the spring deluge. Would it collapse and wash out the road completely?

We passed more dripping trees, and then sloshed to a halt before a porte cochere overhung with black swaying vines. I looked up and didn't believe what I saw—a house of vintage make, certainly no more recent than the early seventeenth century, constructed of some dark wood, huge and square, with porches all around and balconies above the entry.

Light shone dimly from many of the front windows, the only sign of human habitation. Aunt Mellie hurried me out and up the steps, this time leaving Jason to struggle with the bags alone. Dogs somewhere at the rear of the premises burst into furious clamor, rising now and then into mournful howls.

The heavy door creaked. Pressed forward, I drew back involuntarily. I had the strongest urge to run, to bolt. A feeling of terror swept over me, as though once entering this house, I might never leave it.

I took a deep breath, the feeling passed and again prodded impatiently; I stepped inside.

2

I FOUND MYSELF IN THE HALL, a vast, vaulted passageway dimly lit by only a few oil lamps. Beyond and to the right, a door led to what was obviously the library or section of it, and at the far end an immense stair curved to the upper regions, with still more doors opening off the main floor to other parts of the house.

The lack of adequate light bothered me, and I wondered how anyone could find his way about at all. The dimness would take some getting used to. The house was warm, but musty like the interior of the coach. A tall, thin woman I took to be West Indian or Jamaican, glided in and silently took our wraps, then I followed Aunt Mellie into the drawing room.

"Well, say something. What do you think of it?"

"Very nice," I managed. And different, too, a page torn from another era. Unmistakable luxury lay all about me, but it was antiquated—like the ancient, rust-raddled conveyance I'd arrived in and the bent old man who drove it, like this house, like poor little Aunt Mellie herself. I was tired and hungry, and I choked back a wild desire to weep.

Yarn bobbles dangled from lamps, strings of beads from chandeliers; crocheted, knitted, tatted and woven whatnots decorated every table top and mantelpiece.

The room was immense and curtained in dusty red material; there were high-backed pre-Victorian armchairs of the same dusty red plush, with footstools trimmed in faded gold braid.

14

A deep, padded silence pervaded over all. It was almost hypnotic, and I felt that I could have sunk into it had it not been for the searing, nostril-twisting odor of mothballs. But this was the aunts' home. They loved it, and I would show appreciation if it was the last thing I ever did.

Aunt Mellie warmed her blue-veined hands and waited for my further approval.

"Do you recognize anything?" She beamed.

"Only the balconies outside, I think; what I could see of them. I was pretty young, remember, and children generally don't pay much attention to houses. The balcony though— you used to stand out there with your parasol against the sun. I can see you're very comfortable here, but it must have been a tremendous undertaking to have transported anything so far."

"Oh, it was! We did it piece by piece, and had the house constructed as much the same as possible. We had many of these furnishings in England—your father sat upon that very chair, a thoroughly stiff and proper and well-behaved little boy, when he visited with his nanny. I've merely had it recovered; the material that year wore out so badly. Let me see, that was the same year Queen Victoria's son—who was it, William? No, not William. It must have been Edward. Oh dear me, I have my years wrong. At any rate it was the year somebody was supposed to visit Canada." She frowned. "I doubt he did. Anyway I never heard. I had his picture around for a great while. Can't think where it is now. But you'll be wanting dinner."

"I'd like to change first, if I could." My traveling suit was decidedly wrinkled, not to say mud-spattered and damp, and my hair had come down completely. It hung in strings around my shoulders.

Aunt Mellie promptly vetoed my plea. "It is late. We will eat now." She tugged a rope near her elbow, and a bell jangled faintly in the far regions of the house. A young woman in a maid's cap and apron soon appeared.

"We shall want a meal at once," stated Aunt Mellie. "Serve it in the main dining room, with wine. And inform Miss Letitia."

"She retired early. She said you was not to wait for her, that she didn't want anything." The girl glanced nervously at me.

"All right, what's the matter? Get on with it!"

"Well, you see—there's not anything unless you want cold gruel and them mixed-up beans."

"Don't tell me that! There is plenty of food in this house! There has always been plenty of food in this house! What about the roast we had last night? There must be some of that left."

"Cook's in a tither and wouldn't warm it."

Aunt's face suffused with anger. "I'll fix her. I'll discharge her at once!"

The girl stood stolidly. "You can't do that. Why, who would cook the food?"

"You dare presume to tell me what I can and cannot do? I'll have an end to this impertinence. Get something on the table—anything so long as it is fit to eat, and be quick about it!"

Thinking to calm troubled waters, I murmured, "Maybe I'll just run up and say hello to Aunt Lollie, and let her know I'm here."

"You'll do nothing of the sort! When Letitia is in one of her vapors she doesn't want to be disturbed. That girl! Lazy, shiftless creature."

The conclusion of the matter was that the maid was discharged. Jason would take her to the station in the morning, maybe tonight for all I knew. I gathered the cook was something of an autocrat, but, as the more precious commodity, had retained her position. I was to learn later that Cook's temper had ample justification. The real autocrat was Aunt Mellie.

The dining room was large and lighted only by tall candles in a silver candelabra, but I was surprised to see a beautifully appointed table of gleaming mahogany, set with china and silver and crystal, some of which I recognized as extremely valuable heirlooms. The wine decanter was fine cut glass, the dinner service Wedgwood, though chipped, and the linen place mats so worn they barely held together by their hems.

Another girl served, and I caught her stealing curious, lively glances at me from behind my aunt's back. This one was slim, about my own age, with alert brown eyes and a mop of brown curls peeping from beneath her frilly cap.

"Well, don't stand on ceremony," ordered Aunt Mellie and made no apology for the food.

The kidneys were swimming in grease, and I could eat little of them, famished as I was, but the rolls were delicious, and I silently commended the cook, temper notwithstanding, for the delicately browned, feather-light creations. The rolls were accompanied by gooseberry jam, also delicious, and there was cold pudding—not gruel—which almost made up for the lack of the expected roast.

I marveled at my aunt, who continued to be talkative, having completely recovered from her irascibility. The scene in the drawing room remained fresh in my mind, while she appeared to have forgotten all about it. Thus I learned of her lightning-quick changes and the unpredictability of her nature. She could be reasonable one moment and explode into a rage the next.

"Do you leave a young man behind? All girls have young men and I suppose you do as well." She'd spoken abruptly, and oddly enough I could feel her tense, waiting for my reply.

"No. There's nobody, not any more." I shook my head, having another fleeting thought for George, half a world away. After all, the dissolution of even a casual betrothal could be expected to leave a scar or two. So far as I was concerned the last disagreement definitely precluded any hope of reconciliation. George had expected to marry and move in with his mother. It was as simple as that. And

I had come to the conclusion that since Mother held the purse strings—and it was a considerable purse—George would never set sail on his own. I'd never see George again, he'd never come to Canada, I was sure of that. And just as well.

"Good," Aunt Mellie pronounced, and visibly relaxed. "I dislike entanglements." She cleared her throat. "Your accent, you know—" she hesitated, "the English—it does sound nice. You may tell me about England."

I was caught by surprise, but said nothing. She was lonely, was my pitying judgment, and I was again prompted to ask her why, with her money, she didn't return to her homeland if she missed it so much. Instead, I obeyed her request, telling her anything and everything I could think of about England, offering views on current situations, politics and foreign policy, and giving bits of news, even those I was certain she would already have heard, unless Montroth was in another world. But clearly she had not.

She could, when she chose, converse most pleasantly, and I found her a charming mixture of wit and wisdom and naivete. In turn, she regaled me with happenings of her girlhood, of famous visitors "who came to call upon dear Papa who was knighted upon the field of battle, you know." She didn't elaborate upon what field and what battle. Actually her attention span seemed short, and I laid it to the long tiring day just past. At last she dabbed at her lips with a napkin and placed the napkin beside her plate. "Don't feel you must end your meal because of me," she said as she pushed back her chair. "More wine, Lorene?"

"No, thank you." I couldn't have eaten another bite, or drunk anything either.

"I think you will find it pleasant enough here when you become accustomed to us. We have our own ways and dislike change; Letitia and I have lived too long to tolerate change. Except for Letitia's companions, we lead a rather staid existence."

"Companions?" I was puzzled.

A strange expression flitted across Aunt's face. "Not the companions you mean," she said shortly. "Now I think I shall go to bed, I find I am a bit weary." I was surprised she admitted it. All the way out I'd watched for signs of fatigue and had seen none. I was glad I'd had the good sense not to refer to it in connection with her age.

She turned at the door. "Hessit will show you to your room when you are ready. It's the third suite to your left down the hall beyond the head of the stairs. Or if you do not choose to retire yet, feel free to amuse yourself any way you like."

Aunt Mellie took her leave and I headed for the library, anxious to get a good look at my base of operations where I would begin my duties. Books lined the walls, floor to ceiling. At the far end of the room there was a door, evidently kept locked since a chair was placed before it. There were also two or three other chairs, a table, and a worn desk in front of which sat an armchair. Someone had brought in a log to replenish the fire, and the large, high-ceilinged room was still warm. I pulled back the heavy drapery and leaned my forehead against the glass, but nothing was to be seen outside but the driving rain and, beyond, total blackness. At least there hadn't been any further outcry from the dogs. I hoped that meant they were under shelter.

From childhood I'd been surrounded by books, and loved them. As a child, I'd wandered in and out of the Montroth library, but had not taken any real notes of its contents; now, as an adult, I could appreciate what I saw. I was amazed at the number of old titles, leather-bound volumes years out of print and virtually priceless. Keats, Shakespeare, Bolingbroke. I stopped there and lifted the latter down carefully. It opened in my hand, exposing the yellowed flyleaf. *Bolingbroke*, I read, *Henry St. John, Vis.* The Viscount had written a note, in a thin, spidery hand, expressing his gratitude to one Robert Ganning Lewes-Montroth for services rendered, 1720. I knew of Viscount Bolingbroke,

the English statesman and writer, and appreciated what the
gift must have meant, even then. I replaced the volume
carefully and moved on to the next wall.

Here too were gems from yesterday's literary world—
Butler's *Hudibras*, Chaucer's *Canterbury Tales* and a fragile book of poems by Christopher Marlowe. Scores of volumes such as these occupied tier upon tier, interspersed
with romances of more modern ilk and all in helter-skelter
fashion. Aunt Mellie was right, the library was in a terrible
state. I wondered if, at this point, they actually knew what
they did have. Lower shelves presented the same lack of
order; Kipling, an early copy of Darwin, a rather worn
volume by Mendel.

Here was *A History of Occultism*; on impulse I lifted this
from its place and scanned through the index. *Your Fate
and You*, *What the Spirits Say*, *Poisons of Europe and
the East Countries*. Nearby was a well-thumbed volume,
Common Household Poisons Mistaken. Good heavens, I
thought, who was given to entertaining such gloomy subjects? Things that went bump in the night held no interest
for me; of an extremely practical mind, I discredited anything that could not be seen, heard, or felt.

A delicate cough caught my attention. Aunt Mellie had
reappeared—how long had she been standing there in the
doorway watching me?

"Admiring our books?" she murmured, and her puckery
little mouth moved in a tight smile. "I believe ours to be
one of the best collections in the country."

I didn't speak. The curtains behind her swayed as though
a breath of wind had touched them, or a body had recently
passed through; set adrift by the currents in the room, a
new scent rose to mingle with the mothballs. Heliotrope—
there was a distinct odor of heliotrope in the air.

How could Aunt Mellie have changed so quickly and
reappeared like a small genie? Aunt Mellie had retired, or
so she had said. She now stood before me, dressed in a
gown of rusty black that was ruffled at neck and wrists, with

a cameo half as big as my fist on a velvet band around her withered throat. Such dress and such jewelry I had seen in Elizabethan portraits of a great many years ago. The white hair was elaborately coiffed in bouffant curls—or was it a wig? The bone-tiny fingers glittered with rings. There was an air of sweetness and natural shyness that had not been there before.

"Aunt Lollie!" I cried suddenly, "of course! I must have been stupid not to know you!" The likeness was startling; in height and build and facial structure the aunts were almost identical. I'd heard that people who lived together could sometimes grow to resemble one another, but this was ridiculous.

When she displayed no sign of recognition I hastened to add, "I'm Lorene—Lori, your grandniece. You remember I was to come live with you? I just arrived tonight."

"I don't—" She peered closer. "Hand me my glasses, please, there on the table." I obeyed and she settled them on her nose, then started violently. "Lori—it is you! But my dear, you've changed! You're all grown-up, and—my gracious! How many years has it been? You were just a little thing, always losing your jelly bread on the carpet and Millicent scolding you. Come here at once and give your aunt a kiss!"

I did so, my lips brushing her cheek lightly. She held me off to look me over, and I owned to a distinct sense of relief. Here was welcome in plenty.

"Dear me; dear, dear me! Well, after all this time. I'm so glad you came to us, and I hope you will be happy. If there is anything I can do—oh, the candy. I have some bonbons you will particularly like, I think. You favor candy, don't you? Of course, every girl loves bonbons. Would you care for some now? I have a box on my dressing table, I'll get them."

"No, no thanks," I said hastily. "Candy gives me a rash. I've never had much of a sweet tooth. In desserts, yes, but that's enough."

"How—very—odd." Aunt Lollie frowned. "But do be careful about desserts, my love—she often gets me that way."

"She?" I echoed. "Who?"

The old lady hesitated then spread her hands. "Why," she said blandly, "Cook, of course. Who else? Cook often puts in too much flavor, and I am especially sensitive to flavorings." Her head tipped to one side and she surveyed me warmly. "My dear, you are so pretty, and so young. But I'm afraid you'll be lonely here with only two old ladies. There should be a young man for you. Is there a young man? No? Aha, I see your cheeks are pink. You must tell me about it soon. You don't favor your father, you look like your mother. She was a lovely girl! So vibrant. Your hair is truly beautiful, the same sunshine yellow as when you were small. And the complexion! Like milk. The true English complexion. As you see, I try to keep myself up, something my sister does not do! She takes no pride in her appearance at all, any old thing will do for her. That dowdy jacket and horrible knitted bag! I have repeatedly—" She broke off, a spasm crossing her face. "Oh, no," she said. "How could that have happened? I must go," she muttered before I could speak. She swayed, but when I jumped forward to catch her I was curtly waved back. "I can manage!" She clutched the curtains and drew herself up. "Breakfast is— at eight," she gasped. "We would appreciate your being— prompt. My sister does not like to be kept waiting."

I protested, "But at least let me call someone—"

"No!" She fairly spat the word at me. "I want my shawl— hand me my shawl. It has fallen on the floor—there by the chair."

I moved swiftly around the chair, retrieved the shawl, looked up and Aunt Lollie was gone. Instead Hessit stood in the doorway and motioned me to follow her.

Such was my introduction to Montroth, decidedly unusual and not what I expected, but not alarming, either. So far I'd renewed acquaintance with two great-aunts, one testy and often domineering, the other warm and considerate. Aunt Lollie had taken ill from something she'd eaten; I'd thought it more serious but according to Aunt Mellie, she was prone to such upsets and had probably only left her bed too soon.

None of it was frightening, I told myself as I followed the woman up the stairs and to my door. Why should I feel uneasy? The foreboding, the dark currents which had possessed me at the moment I entered these doors, were all pure fantasy.

ᖇᖇ 3 ᖇᖇ

MY SUITE WAS LAVISH—more bobbles, more bangles, threadbare Oriental carpets which a half century ago would have been gorgeous and the same heavy-to-the-floor window hangings. On a marble-topped Vecci table was a pitcher and bowl. The lower section of a commode housed an ornate chamber pot with its lid discreetly sweatered in knit. The convenience fascinated me. I had never seen one quite like it, and knew I'd hesitate using it.

The bathroom was extremely innovative, and I viewed with some awe the network of pipes and pull chains. A copper hot-water heater had already been lighted with matches from a nearby tin tray. Dark brown paint covered the board floor and the tub stood high and sturdy on its four claw feet. Everything in Aunt Mellie's house would be sturdy, I reflected, but antiquated or no, I couldn't help appreciating the love and dedication to home which could provide creature comforts in a place like Montroth.

A soak in the tub did wonders, and when I toweled off at last and slipped into my frilly nightdress, I felt worlds better. My bags had been unpacked and my clothing neatly hung in the big double closets. A fire burned cheerily in the grate to keep the room warm and cozy. Poor Jason, if he has to supply all this wood, I thought. But he probably had help. After all, this was a big household and must require many servants to maintain it.

Once in bed, sleep eluded me, my mind sifting through the events of the day. Stephen Landrau. Even though our

24

time together was so brief, it was like an awakening. Was it the same for him? Aunt Mellie's cool welcome, almost as if she regretted my coming. Aunt Lollie's warm one. The ridiculous tooth-and-claw relationship between them, two old ladies spatting with each other like ineffectual kittens. The reason, of course, being too many years of living in close proximity, too narrow an outlook. It was a wonder they weren't at each other's throats!

The name Venson kept recurring to me, Werner Venson. Aunt had mentioned it but where else had I seen it? Then I remembered. In Vancouver I had bought a newspaper and scanned through it briefly while waiting for Aunt Mellie. There had been a small notice referring to a Werner Venson, who was still missing and presumed lost in the interior of British Columbia. The search had been abandoned. Aunt Mellie said he'd been at Montroth. A pity, I concluded, with an involuntary shiver as I recalled the depth of those forests, that he couldn't have been persuaded to remain here, or that he ever came this far in the first place.

My thoughts went into a sudden plunge as the dogs erupted with such fury I was sure they'd tackled something and were tearing it to pieces. The uproar continued for several minutes, subsiding finally into snarls and the snarls into barking. At last that, too, ceased. I tried to tell myself that those corridors of timber were nearby and the dogs had probably heard something, a wild animal perhaps. When my heart quit hammering and I was able to settle down, I pulled the covers over my head and went to sleep.

Some time later I woke with a start. It was well past midnight, I judged from the chill in the room, most likely along toward morning. I lay still in my warm little nest, trying to orient myself and wondering what had wakened me. The lamp which I had forgotten to blow out had nearly burned dry, the flame dim and the blackened wick sending up smelly little twists of smoke. I muttered an impatient word and rose to extinguish it, then halted to listen. There was movement outside my door, and as I watched, the hair on the back of my neck rising, the knob slowly turned.

Instinct moved me behind that door, a heavy poker snatched from the fireplace in my hand, but the knob slowly slipped back to its original position. The door wasn't locked since there was no key and it had not occurred to me that I needed one, so why hadn't the would-be intruder carried out his intention? There was a soft sound on the carpeting as footsteps faded down the hall, and I lowered my weapon, feeling a trifle foolish. Here I was, poised to bash somebody over the head, and I'd been in this house only a few hours!

Yet, if it had been Aunt Lollie, why hadn't she knocked or simply entered? She would have known I was asleep. Even more ridiculous to suspect grim-lipped little Aunt Mellie of creeping about the halls; she would have entered if she'd pleased, if she had to batter the door down to do it. I knew no one else in this establishment.

I went back to bed but not to sleep; an hour or so later I rose and dressed, this time to peer out of the window into a glorious morning. It was still early and the sun not yet up over the tops of the trees. And there were trees! Never in all my life had I seen so many or so huge. My room overlooked the narrow drive; across it was an impenetrable wall of heavy green. As far as I could see from the window there was forest. Was Montroth surrounded by it, trapped by trees, immense greedy giants which held their secrets jealously, resisted light, air, warmth, laughter?

It was a sobering thought, and I decided it was time to go downstairs. I'd donned a dark blue morning skirt, a white waist with a tie at the throat, and my hair, brushed smooth, was caught up with a narrow blue ribbon.

As I pulled the door open something dropped to the floor, a scrap of paper which had not been there when I entered the room last night, nor when Hessit brought me upstairs!

It was rough foolscap of the sort children used in school, with a crude penciled warning scrawled on it as if in haste. *Go from here now*, it read, the "now" underlined. *Danger to you. Go or you will be killed.* The "killed" had been crossed out and the word "next" substituted. *Go now or you will be next.*

Next what, to be killed? I don't believe this, I muttered; maybe in some sensational melodrama, but not here and not now, in the modern nineteenth century. Was it some kind of crude practical joke? I crumpled the paper with fingers gone suddenly nerveless and dropped it to the floor, then scooped it up again and spread it out for closer inspection. It was unsigned of course, with an almost foreign word usage that could have been feigned to mask the identity of the sender.

Who else could it be for, but myself? Montroth had been an established household long before my arrival, I was the newcomer, it had to be meant for me. In that case, who could have sent such a thing? I had no enemies here or anywhere else as far as I knew, so who would want to harm me? And even if I'd been so minded, which I was not, how could I be expected to leave? It wasn't that easy—a fact of which the writer of the note must have certainly been aware. As remote as Montroth was, I had no idea how to return to civilization. Whoever wrote this warning, I told myself as I felt my anger rise, must be stupid to think I could be routed in such fashion. I had a right to be here and no note was going to change my mind. Still angry, I flattened it and thrust it under a linen dresser scarf, and after snatching up my sweater, left the room.

Hallway and stairs were still dim in the early morning light, but nearing the lower floor, I could hear movement somewhere out back. With no notion of where I was going, I threaded my way through the rooms, an empty dining alcove, what had obviously at one time been an attached sunroom, to find myself at last facing another hallway and a door. This led to a porch. A figure stood at the end, back to me and involved with utensils on a table. She wore a long black dress with an equally long apron. I saw pans, bowls, and pitchers with young hands working over them, and some sort of framework into which was being poured yellow soupy liquid from a pitcher.

I stepped around where I could see. It was the girl who had served dinner last night. "What are you doing?"

She looked up, recognized me and smiled, then she made a face. "Making candles."

"With that?" I pointed.

"Beeswax. This little contraption—" she indicated what appeared to be a charcoal burner, "melts it, then it is poured and left to cool. These strings here are—but you don't want to know about all this stuff, do you? I don't have any tea but do you want some coffee? I have a break coming. I've been at this since five."

I smiled back. "I certainly do. I have been wondering where I could find something hot to drink. Do we go inside?"

"No." She leaned forward conspiratorially. She had short dark curls, and dark eyes in a piquant face. Young, vibrant; she'd be candid and a little brash, and I liked her. "If I do, Narcisse will be at me for something else. That's the cook. She's a slave driver. Right now, she's mad at everybody and everything. You're lucky."

I thought of the note and sighed. This girl hadn't left it, I was sure.

Her name was Belinda Fourier and she was from a village up north, working at Montroth for the summer to help out. There were eight children at home and she was the eldest. I asked how long she had been here.

"I came in March, but I'm not sure I'll stay. Too far out." Her nose wrinkled. "Sometimes this place gives me the creeps, especially when those dogs are howling their heads off."

She found two cups, dragged two stools from beneath the table, and we sat down to consume our steaming brew in companionable fashion. She looked me over frankly. "You're the brightest thing to hit this place in a month of Sundays. I like your outfit. It becomes you. Look at me. The wax spatters and I don't dare get it all over my own clothes. Lord knows who wore this shroud before me." She picked up a fold of the skirt and let it drop. "Ugh—black."

I laughed. "How many are there here?"

"You mean servants? Seven, no, six after Doris went." Belinda giggled. "Doris is my second cousin, but nobody knew that—a good worker but a little on the slow side. I told her to just keep her mouth shut, speak when she was spoken to, and not say anything otherwise except yes and no. But I couldn't get it through her head. She was bound to go on explaining and she was axed. You can't argue with—you can't talk back to your employers. What part of England are you from?"

I told her Sussex, and we chatted amiably for a time. Then I said, "You mentioned the dogs. I'm curious about them. Is there a caretaker to feed them?"

"Haines," the girl said after a swallow of coffee. "He's not very bright, harmless though, and real nice if you don't mind that sort of thing. He's old."

"Jason?"

The girl frowned and shrugged. "Same, I guess. But kind. I don't know about Jason. An accident, somebody said. It sure left him all crippled up, whatever happened. And then there's a—but I better let you find that out for yourself."

Mentally I counted on my fingers. Doris, at least slightly incompetent; the man who took care of the dogs, not too bright; Jason, mute and I didn't know how intelligent. I wouldn't have judged philanthropy to be my aunts' strong point, I thought, then felt mean.

I drained the last of my cup. "Well, I like animals, but I've never heard such racket. I don't see how anyone gets any sleep around here. It must be hard on older people who need their rest."

"I guess yes, especially when they don't even belong to the place."

I looked at her, puzzled. "The dogs don't? But whose are they, then?"

The girl frowned. "Oh, some fellow left 'em here. Funny, too. If he brought them why didn't he take them with him when he went? You'd think he'd want to. Or why didn't he come back after them? He just disappeared between dark and daylight—here one day and gone the next."

For some reason icy fingers touched my spine. "But who was he?"

Belinda shrugged. "Said his name was Owens, at least that was what was noised around. But you know how servants talk. He was here a month, I understand, but that was before my time so I don't know the straight of it. The dogs are supposed to be vicious. The old—Miss Millicent and Miss Letitia are both frightened to death of them—Miss Millicent especially."

Aunt Mellie terrified of the dogs? Aunt Mellie terrified of anything was hard to believe. If it were true, why then had she kept them? Watchdogs were not uncommon. Many English manors maintained such animals for protection, and I supposed it was perfectly natural, this far out.

"More coffee?"

I nodded and held out my cup. She filled it and her own, and reseated herself. "What do you do to stay alive?"

I laughed. In this mausoleum, she might have said. "Me? I'll be busy in the library, straightening up the books. Cataloguing them."

"That won't take the rest of your life. What are you going to do after?"

"Well—I'm supposed to be living here, at least that was the understanding. The aunts are old and can't go on forever living by themselves."

Belinda tapped her cup with one stubby little fingernail. Then she looked up, for the moment sober. "You're not offended."

"What for?" I said. "No. Of course not." But I knew what she meant.

She shrugged. "You're different than most. Here I'm rattling on, ordinarily I wouldn't even be talking to you.

You're of the Manor and I'm not. Ma always said I was too forward, that I should remember my station. But I figure you're going to be lonesome in this place even with all you've got to do, and I know I am without even anybody near my own age to talk to."

I smiled. She was right of course. And I wasn't offended. How could I be? She was natural and outgoing and fun; besides, I'd never been stuffy that way.

"Go on. You were saying—?"

"All right. It's about Joe. You'd like Joe—he's wonderful. My man friend. He works in a general store, clerking. You got one—a man friend, I mean?"

I felt a smile curve my lips. "I don't think you could call him that. We only saw each other once."

"But fireworks?" My companion dimpled. She was charming. "Sometimes all it takes is once. Believe me, I know. That's the way it was between Joe and me, and it's never quit. We've been walking out together a year and it'll be another year before we can get married. What's your friend's name?"

"Stephen Landrau," I murmured and added dreamily, "I'd like to see him again."

"Nobody left back in England?"

It was the second time I had been asked that. She was curious, but it went with her nature and I didn't mind. "No. I was betrothed but broke it off."

"So you scuttled him," Belinda observed wisely. "You must have had your reasons. Good to get things like that settled before coming to a new land. And if sparks flew like you say, you can bet your Stephen Landrau will be around. Don't you think?"

"I hope so. If he can find me."

"If he wants to bad enough, he will. And I'd bet you could be pretty certain of it."

There was one thing more I had to know. "About last night," I said bluntly. "Would you have any idea what set off the dogs?"

Belinda's shoulders tightened, she became suddenly diffident. "No. A skunk, maybe, or a deer blundered through the garden and they caught the scent. You never know what will do it. We had one once, a big Collie that used to sit by the gate and wait for the moon to come up so he could yowl himself hoarse. Well," she said, "I suppose I'd better be getting on with my job or I'll really have Narcisse down on me."

I stood up too. "It was nice talking to you," I said and meant it. "I would like to do it again."

She grinned, the curls tumbling down over her forehead. "Sure, if you don't mind hobnobbing with a menial."

I smiled as I walked away, but I was to remember our conversation and puzzle over it. The dogs were not vicious; something had set them off; Aunt Mellie was terrified of them. And even stranger, why the less than normal help?

4

REMEMBERING AUNT LOLLIE'S ADVICE, I was prompt for breakfast. There were only the two of us at the huge table, Aunt Mellie at one end and myself at the other, with a yawning expanse of mahogany in between. I hoped to find her in a pleasant mood, for I meant to suggest a key to my apartments, and I had no idea how she would react.

Unfortunately, with the complete about-face I was coming to expect, she was curt to the point of rudeness, speaking seldom and grudgingly. Her sister, she reported with no wasted words, was still incapacitated with her upset.

"I saw her last night," I said, thinking to warm the chill atmosphere.

"You are mistaken! Letitia is sick, I tell you. She cannot leave her bed." The old lady stared at me coldly over her glasses.

I was left with the choice of agreeing to a falsity, or supporting what I knew to be true. I chose the latter. "She was in the library," I heard myself say gently. "She came there and welcomed me. She was very warm and gracious. We chatted for some time, reminiscing. She took sick there."

It was a mistake. Aunt glared. It was becoming clear to me that if I wished to exist amicably in this house I would do well not to mention the name of one sister to the other. Each time they did so themselves, it was always as a declaration of war.

Doggedly, realizing the futility of tact, I broached my subject, not, however, mentioning the note. "There was someone at my door last night. The episode frightened me half to death. May I have a key to my quarters? I confess I would feel safer."

"Someone trying to enter your rooms?" Aunt Mellie snorted. "Nonsense! I want you to know no one prowls *my* halls. There are no ghosts here, no goblins. You are imagining things."

"I heard it," I maintained, still patiently, but with undaunted persistence. "I wouldn't have told you had I not done so. I am not easily frightened. I am not given to foolish fancies as you seem to imply. There *was* someone at my door last night, I distinctly heard movement against the paneling; the floor creaked and as I watched, the knob turned. Now do I get that key?"

There was grudging admiration in the old lady's eyes. "You've got spunk, I will say that for you. If Milton had had half your gumption he'd never—no matter! I'll see you get your key. But you need not be afraid, what you heard was merely Hessit about to enter with an extra blanket for your bed. She feared you might be cold."

I was astonished. Hessit dropping notes? It seemed logical, didn't it, that whoever was at the door had left the paper? But *Hessit*? It didn't make sense. "If it was Hessit," I asked practically, "why didn't she speak out? Say something, at least knock?"

"She suspected you might be uneasy in a strange place," Aunt Mellie snapped, "and did not wish to frighten you further. She senses these things. I told her to forget it, deciding it best that she wait until you asked, rather than give you nightmares by going into your room. Some people are offensively squeamish."

I reserved judgment. What would she say if she was aware of the note? Nevertheless, if the part about the blanket were true, I could appreciate the thoughtfulness and said so. "I'm sorry. But I wish she'd let me know."

Aunt said nothing, her thin lips pinched tight as though in displeasure or bad temper, or both. I had the good sense not to press further and, ignoring the impasse, bent my head to my plate.

Hessit served, never once acknowledging my presence. I might have been invisible for all the notice she took of me. I searched the dark face but it was blank, impassive. Silent as a mummy, she slipped in with hot muffins and sausages—and excellent too—slipping out with the silver teapot on the tray, only to reappear almost at once with the vessel replenished. She looked neither right nor left, spoke not a word.

Aunt pushed back her plate, but did not rise. She regarded me coolly. "You had something more to say. A complaint. Then get it out in the open. You don't like it here, can't stand it. What else?"

I was startled and, for a moment, taken aback. "This country is—different, of course. I think one of the hardest things to become accustomed to is the fact that we seem to be completely surrounded by forest. It appears so— overwhelming."

Aunt Mellie nodded briefly. "Well—yes, I should say these tall trees could seem a bit overwhelming to a new-comer. But you need not be concerned with the forest, need not go into it nor have anything to do with it, and of course one does not venture into the trees at night. I shouldn't like that, myself, and I have lived here many years. In Montroth we have a warm, bright refuge, full of all the comforts of home. Therefore we do not wander. But you said becoming adjusted to the trees is one of the difficult things you find you must become accustomed to. What is the other?"

In her stiff, blunt way, was she trying to be kind? I hoped so and replied warmly. "It's only that we're so isolated. I'm used to having more people about."

Aunt cut me off with a sharp gesture. "We have no need of such distractions. I told you. We have no problem with *our* lives. You have left someone behind and are mooning over him."

"Good heavens, no!" I burst out laughing. "No, not at all. Nothing like that. I just thought—"

"Don't. As for people, I told you there are occasional visitors. Over the years, quite a few. I told you that, too. Mr. Owens—Harold Owens—his are the dogs you hear out back, uncontrollable beasts!—was with us for some time, almost two months, it was, if I remember correctly. He had to leave quite suddenly, to go back to India. He has extensive holdings there. Sad when he had to go, but such a lonely person. Dreadful when there is no one. Almost no use living."

"Oh, I don't think that," I said quickly. "There is always light somewhere, if one looks long enough for it. He'll find it."

"A nice philosophy," Aunt conceded, "though not always accurate. In Mr. Owens' case, certainly not so. When one must turn to dogs for companionship—"

"It's too bad they have to be kept penned. Perhaps I can make friends with them," I suggested eagerly. "I like animals very much and they seem to like—"

"Oh no, I wouldn't!" Aunt Mellie cried at once. "No, it wouldn't be safe. Truly you mustn't go near them! Letitia or I never dare. One can't tell what they would do! We have a man who takes care of them—he feeds them. I still cannot think why I—" She broke off agitatedly, and I nodded to reassure her. I saw with surprise that the old lady was genuinely terrified; she'd given a visible shudder and her little face had gone suddenly pinched and white. It seemed inconceivable to me. I had always had a natural kinship with animals, dogs especially.

"Of course," I soothed gently, "I understand." But surely Aunt was exaggerating—the unreasoning fear a quirk of hers, resulting perhaps from some fright as a child? As soon as possible I would like to have a look at those animals myself.

"Ah, well, I don't mean to get so upset. But those vicious creatures always upset me! I should have had them put away when Mr. Owens left, instead of troubling with them the way I do. They're devious. They look at one with big yellow eyes, like ghouls. If I were superstitious I could even believe—but no matter. That barking, that howling! It is the howling I cannot stand, it sounds as if it comes from the grave! Like dispossessed souls, prowling the earth. I do fear them. Sometimes I think they are not animals at all, but humans in animal form—"

"But that is absurd," I said steadily. "They are only animals, of course. Perhaps if you once got acquainted with them—"

"Not I! Never!"

I sighed. "Mr. Owens couldn't take them with him?"

"Well—hardly."

"He will perhaps be back after them, then?"

Aunt Mellie abruptly chuckled, once more all smiles and bobbing curls and sweet laughter. "Oh, I doubt that, I really do. But why waste time talking about them—such a distressing subject. Now I shall excuse myself. Do not feel you have to get into hard work at once, go about the House, get acquainted with it, explore its secret passages."

"It has secret passages?" For some reason this didn't please me much. A big gloomy place with secret passages . . .

"Oh my, yes. Most interesting, and to one not familiar with the twists and turns, they could be most confusing. Just pay attention to which direction you are going, and where you came from, and you'll be fine. We had them built especially as escape routes should we wish them. Now do take all the time you want."

She rose with a curt nod, and the meal was finished, the conversation done. I'd opened my mouth to voice the expected question, escape from what? but hadn't the chance. Certainly there was no one within untold miles to do them harm. Another quirk, and I supposed they were entitled to those.

I'd have liked to look in on ailing little Aunt Lollie but decided against it. Better let well enough alone. Still, if she didn't put in an appearance soon, I would disobey orders and go see her anyway. My allegiance was no more to one than the other. Now, with all quiet again at nine in the morning I could get busy on the library, though I'd been given no specific instructions. But first I'd have a look around.

No one was about, and mistaking a turn I wound up in the morning room, took a wrong turn once again only to blunder into a closed-off alcove piled with dusty, broken furniture. I retraced my steps into the connecting hallway, traversed that, and came finally into a large and drafty building off the main house which seemed to be an unused conservatory.

It was a dead place. No plants grew here. The many windows were dusty and hung with spiders and their webs; the ever-greedy vines, whatever they were, clambered up the walls and scratched dry fingers against the glass.

"What," I muttered impatiently, "have I gotten myself into?" A crackly tendril of some long-extinct plant clutched at my clothing and I pulled it off sharply. The earthen container fell to the floor, but didn't break. As carefully as I could, lest there still be some remote spark of life remaining in the battered stalk, I scooped up earth and plant and replaced them.

It was then I noticed the leather folder lying half covered with earth. Picking it up gingerly I saw it was a wallet, gold-stamped with the initials S.S. My first impulse was to put it back where it came from exactly as I found it, but it was moldy and green around the edges and fell open in my hand. A wallet was a personal possession one carried with him at all times, wasn't it? It held cards, letters, identification? Yet this one contained nothing of the sort. Disappointed, I carefully folded the limp thing back together and made my way out of the place. Outside, I simply tucked it under a convenient bush to be retrieved upon my return to the house. One of the aunts would know whose it was.

The next moment I looked around, marveling. It was as I had suspected. From where I now stood at the rear of the place, I could see that the entire estate was encircled by trees. A hole might have been scooped out of the dense timber, and house and grounds dropped into it. There were no neighbors, never had been neighbors, the few signs of civilization all Montroth's own. *Settle in*, Aunt Mellie had said, and that's all I could do. Settle in and get used to it. There was an orchard with gnarled trees and a cluster of outbuildings in various states of disrepair, a berry patch beyond, and nearer the woods a garden, but that was all.

Directly in my path was a far more ancient garden spot, long abandoned and overgrown with weeds and brush. I entered a gate sagging on rusty hinges and saw that in one corner of this compound the native dark evergreens grew especially lush and green. From this corner I caught the sound of someone moaning, crying—or singing?

I halted where I was, keenly mindful of that open gate behind me, and escape. "Who is it?" I called guardedly. There was no reply but the aimless humming ceased at once.

"Hello," I said again and waited, but there was still no response. I moved forward to the sudden alarmed scurry of something gray, or gray-blue, slipping between the trunks of the trees. My scalp crept, but I held my ground. One of the servants of course, it had to be! "Who's there?"

"Ana."

A slight figure stepped forward hesitantly, bucket in hand, and my breath went out of me in a long sigh. It was only a scullery girl, at her task of emptying garbage.

"Ana. Oh, I am sorry. Did I frighten you?"

The girl, who could not have been more than thirteen, and a small thirteen at that, seemed disinclined to talk. Indian, all or part, swarthy of skin and with hair in a long ragged braid down her back, she stood in her dark work dress, pail in hand, and undecided. "I guess," she said at last.

"I'm Lori," I said, "Lorene Kilmer. I've come to live here at Montroth with my aunts." For a moment the girl gave no indication she understood, then her eyes widened. She managed an "Oh," and turned at a call from the other side of the shrubbery.

"Ana!" Belinda's mop of black curls thrust above the bushes. "Oh, I didn't see you there," she said to me. Then to the girl, "Narcisse says to quit dawdling—one chore needn't take all day. Where did you dump that garbage, anyway? You know that's not the right place. You're supposed to bury it in the orchard. You know that."

"But I—but—"

"All right, go on now. It's already done but next time better do it right."

"I—I—but I am—" The girl looked fearfully toward the bright, sunlit orchard. "I go," she gurgled, clutched her bucket and scurried off, not looking back.

Belinda stepped out, offering a big grin and a shake of the head. "I just came to see what was keeping Ana. You look real nice—sunshine on your hair. I'm stuck indoors today. Cook's orders."

"Doing what?"

Belinda's nose wrinkled. "A little bit of everything. Then, laundry. Today is laundry day. There's a little stream comes from farther back in the woods, and a shed. The washing stuff is in there. Which way did you come?"

I smiled too. Her good humor was infectious. "Through the house. I got lost twice, then I'd had enough, at least for right now. Isn't it wonderful, so warm out."

"Great. I'd like to stay and enjoy it with you but Narcisse will be yelling pretty soon. I give her about three minutes, then a pan will crash or she'll yell. What are you up to?"

"The library, I guess. I probably should be at it right now but couldn't resist getting about a bit."

"Sure, I don't blame you. Scratching around with dusty books would drive me crazy, but I suppose somebody's got to do it." Again the impish grin. "Know what? You just could be hearing from your Stephen one of these days."

"Why, how could I hear?" I asked in astonishment, then remembered; my father had written, hadn't he? Then there was the reply inviting me to Montroth.

"Jason drives down once in a while and collects what mail there is, usually when he goes out to get supplies. Which," she added with a grimace, "isn't often I must admit. It's plenty of good hard miles to Outside—that's what we call it up here. You remember getting to Montroth, so you know. Have you seen the dogs yet?"

I shook my head and she pointed out a path. "Just follow that and it'll lead you right to the pens. Haines will be there, and he sure won't mind. Probably be glad for the company, he doesn't get to see many people."

"You don't mean he's a—prisoner?"

"No, nothing like that. Of course not. But taking care of the dogs is his job, and it's what he does."

"But where—" I was puzzled, "does he stay nights? I mean, where does he live?"

"In a little shack behind the pens. Same with Jason. You noticed the barn and stables? Jason has a place off one corner of the barn. There's a lean-to attached to the stables where harness and stuff like that is kept. You'll get used to the place—"

There was the crash of tin and "Belinda!" came in a raucous bawl from the house. I felt guilty. That would be the ruler of the kitchens, Narcisse. With a wave of her hand back over her shoulder, Belinda was gone.

Again heavy shrubbery stood in my path and I made my way carefully around it, giving plenty of leeway to a pile of brush and old boards. I'd taken several steps before I heard wood cracking, a thick, muffled sound, and felt something sinking underfoot, but so gradually I took it to be only the unevenness of the ground. Then all at once my feet encountered nothing but empty air. I threw out my arms, clutching wildly, but I was falling, falling, with a scream choked back in my throat.

I landed with a mighty thud and in swirls of choking dust, with the wind near knocked out of me. But my heart pumped solidly, breath began to follow regular breath, and I did not seem to be hurt. My legs were all of a piece—nothing broken there; my arms belonged. I sat for a time where I was, marveling at my lack of injury and trying to adjust my eyes to the surroundings. From what could be seen in the still swirling dimness, I'd broken through the roof of an old cellar, landing fortunately on a pile of dry earth and dead leaves, which had drifted down from some earlier cave-in. Above was a tiny patch of blue sky and the ragged edges of the hole through which I had tumbled.

Nearby was what seemed to be a heap of old clothing—it was impossible to make out what the individual garments might be, and seven or eight pairs of men's shoes arranged in an orderly array. Castoffs? Of course, the place had evidently been used as a dumping ground for such things. I got to my feet gingerly and rubbed my bruises. Only luck would have kept the roof from collapsing before. Anyone could have fallen through it and been hurt badly. Hours, days, could go by until I was found—maybe years! This subterranean grotto was certainly unused, the patina of dirt which lay thick everywhere proved that.

My vision clearing, I could make out other vague shapes in the gloom. In the corners the dusk was deeper, and from somewhere out of those depths came a shuffling sound. I whirled toward that sound and instinctively backed away, coming up hard against an immovable object behind me. It was a bench, and beyond it was a heap of broken chairs. A stack of barrels and half barrels made a dim pile in one of the corners, another wall was lined with more barrels, yet strangely enough these were free of dust.

There was another scurrying sound and then still another from different points of the room. Rats! They were all around me, the cellar was full of them. My skin crawled and I felt panic rising. I whirled and ran to the opposite side of the room as far away as I could, fear mounting that there might not be any escape. I looked longingly at the scrap of blue sky overhead but I'd fallen too far, it was impossible to climb back out of the hole. One could never have done it, even with a ladder, and there was no ladder.

Something soft and yielding brushed my ankles and a scream gurgled in my throat. Again I fled to the opposite side of my prison, bumping blindly into ancient crates and boxes and routing up a whole new set of scurryings. Rats, I told myself, that's all they were, and gulped down my revulsion. They were as afraid of me, I insisted, as I was of them; I had invaded their territory, not they mine.

Sound and movement increased. The inhabitants of this underground hotel were growing bolder, and from a pile of litter I caught up a chunk of board and prepared to defend myself. I scrambled up on a wobbly bench, and braced myself against a shelf. Behind me a large jug of some kind toppled to the floor with a crash. An overpoweringly pungent, irritating odor slowly rose to permeate the air, a smell totally unidentifiable. I coughed, choking. I had to get out of here! The entire wall was lined with shelves, the shelves loaded with innumerable bottles, jugs and jars. But they, like the barrels, did not seem unused. Even on the floor, the jagged pieces of glass catching the light from above sparkled cleanly.

I coughed again and my eyes smarted. The fumes were evidently getting to the inmates too, for abruptly a large gray shape broke from his dusky shelter and skittered across the floor, then another, the last pausing beneath the bench, sniffing, with its forefeet raised. I gritted my teeth. "Either me or you," I muttered and hit it with a whack. The board shattered, and I threw it from me as far as I could. I avoided looking at my victim.

Straining my eyes for a possible means of exit, my heart leaped—a door! There was a set of stairs behind this pile of

junk and a door at the top leading to heaven knew where—
it didn't matter so long as it was *out*.

I began clawing at the pile, unconscious of my bruised
hands and torn nails. My hair fell across my face and I
whipped it back impatiently. The pile half-leveled at last,
and I climbed over the remainder. Finally my feet were
on steps, solid steps. I'd lost a shoe in the skirmish and
my stockinged toe struck a sharp metal object—a barrel
hoop, I found when I picked it up. It was narrow but I
hoped, strong. If it didn't work at least I had the heel of
the other shoe.

I pounded on the door with the hoop and yelled at the
top of my lungs, but there was no answer. It was like being
trapped in a crypt! The thought gave no comfort. I beat
wildly upon the door with my shoe, then the hoop, and then
once more the shoe, then dropped the shoe and concentrated
on the hoop. The door was of some heavy material and as
immovable as the Rock of Gibraltar. Fumes swirled about
the place, though they seemed a little less strong, and tears
still streamed down my cheeks. At least the pandemonium
had scattered the rats, all save one. He was investigating
his fallen comrade; my stomach churning, I aimed the shoe
at him.

I sank to the steps, exhausted. What now? Think back.
Think straight. There were hinges; doors, to be doors, had
to have hinges and locks. They were the closures, but they
were also openers. I felt suddenly ashamed of myself, aware
that if I'd stopped batting about indiscriminately and instead
used my common sense—Father always said I had enough
of it to get by in any pinch if I chose to use it—I might have
made more headway. I got to my feet, clutching my hoop.

I never knew how long I worked, only how hard. A sliver
pierced one of my fingers, and I tore it out, neatly, with my
teeth, dropping the hoop. In bending to retrieve it, I gained
another splinter, this time in the heel of my hand, and let
this one go. I'd earlier sustained a scratch on my arm from
a wire on a crate; still another sliver from another crate

grazed my cheek. My hair was tangled and dust-stiffened about my face. I'd not allowed myself to consider failure, that bars and spikes and massive planks might ultimately defeat me. I only knew there must be a means of escape and I had to try.

Concentrating on the lock side of the huge door, I felt it give at last and muttered my thanks aloud. Even if it opened into some remote and forgotten corner of the house, at least it was freedom. When the monstrous barrier finally crashed before me—and it opened into the kitchens—I gulped in great hungry mouthfuls of fresh rejuvenating air, and fell on bloodied knees.

Cook took one look at this apparition, threw up her arms, and bolted.

༄ 5 ༄

"GOOD GRACIOUS, CHILD," Aunt Lollie cried, "you might have been killed!"

"I might have, at that," I retorted grimly. Didn't she know of the cellar, that the roof was in dangerous condition and could have caved in at any moment and at the slightest pressure? But the old lady's agitation was genuine.

"And you hurt yourself, too! Scratched—dear me, that is too bad! But not deep, though, praise be. Now the one on your cheek—lean forward and let me see. Gracious, I am sorry. We should have boarded that place up long ago. Now I wonder why we didn't. Wasn't there a door? There must have been a door. Then why did you go through the roof? Oh, I see. The door was blocked and you fell. But the roof—oh my, I have forgotten how it was built, it was so long ago. One simply goes on expecting things to last forever. We needed that cellar. In its way, it was very necessary." Aunt Lollie waved a hand vaguely. "At any rate, you should not have to suffer for . . ." She sighed. "The dress, you say it was torn. It can be mended. Hessit can do that. She is clever with the needle. Just ask her. Or you can borrow one of mine."

Black bombazine and pink lace, purple velvet and ornamental braid, or would it be feathers? Aunt Lollie was given to feathers, the frothier the better, ostrich her favorite. Or maribou. It was a generous offer, but by no stretch of the imagination could I feature myself in one of her gowns.

I was stiff and sore, but that was all. The experience seemed to have done me no harm and, other than fingernails which would take a bit of time to grow back, and the scratches on arm and cheek, I was little the worse for wear. When Aunt Lollie had cried out in horror and shed real tears at my experience, I'd assured her I healed fast and that she was not to worry. I was fine. The greatest bruise, I added, was to my pride; if I'd kept my head as I should have done, I would have broken out of my prison far sooner.

"But you are so self-reliant," Aunt Lollie commended. "I cannot see myself in such a fix—I'm sure *I* wouldn't have known what to do!"

Facing the other half of the sisterly duo was quite another story. Aunt Mellie was furious. When she heard of it she raised an uproar that rattled the mansion; she had Jason out within minutes, boarding up the hole.

"There is a proper door into that cellar," she pointed out sharply, "that door was closed and meant to remain so. I told you to get acquainted with Montroth, not cause damage or become involved in situations like this."

"I'm sure I—"

She cut me off. "What were you doing bumbling about in the area anyway?"

I felt myself stiffen at the accusations, so completely unexpected, and I held my temper with an effort. "I am being blamed for an *accident*? I had gone for a walk and was returning to the house. A pile of brush and boards was in my way, I moved around it. It is not my fault the roof was rotten, nor did I mean to step on it. I would not have gone that way if I had. There were a million rats down there—"

"Rats!"

"That's it. Rats."

Aunt drew herself up. "There are no rats in my cellar!"

"There were, and are," I replied firmly. "Somebody should clear them out before they spread to the rest of the house. Or maybe they already have. Have you been down there lately? Dust like you'd never believe—years of dust. And barrels and all sorts of junk—"

Aunt impaled me with a vindictive glare. "Well, what did you expect, crystal and linen table service? I do not employ butlers or guides to show stupid girls the way around my cellars. You should keep out of a place like that; you ought to have more sense than to go poking about where you've no right to be!"

The sarcasm was cruel and the dressing-down both spiteful and unnecessary, and I wondered, with justifiable resentment, what the clamor was all about. One would think she cared more that her precious storehouse had been entered than that someone had tumbled through the roof to the peril of life and limb. It was on the tip of my tongue to say so, but arguing wouldn't have done any good, and so contented myself with merely asking curiously, "What was in that jug I broke, anyway? It smelled horrible, stung my nose and eyes, it was so strong."

"Bug-spray," snapped the old lady. Her brittle inspection riveted me. "And if it's any of your business, disinfectant for the dog pens. What happened served you right. Don't go in there again."

I stared at her. "Don't worry. I won't." I watched her march from the room, her little jaw set and her back very straight. Would there be more such altercations, or was this an isolated instance?

The library was my retreat. Sorting, examining, and listing always relaxed me. This morning I pushed the table up near the wall and each volume was noted as to title, author, publisher, and date of publication. My final notes were entered into one of two ancient ledgers found in the drawer of the desk. There was very little to work with otherwise— a box of inexpensive lead pencils, a pen in a wooden holder and a few extra points, old-fashioned bottles of black ink— these were my tools.

The old titles claimed me, and almost every moment I unearthed new treasures. Keats, Mallory and Cicero leaned companionably shoulder to shoulder with an early English translated version of Lucian's *Dialogues of the Dead*, with a copy of *Discourses on Early Roman History* thrown in for good measure. I loved the rich scent of the old volumes, the pebbly feel of the leather beneath my fingers, the sense of being in touch with the past and the great minds which had frequented it. And here in the quiet, with only my own thoughts for company, I seemed to feel Stephen near. The illusion was so strong at times that I turned, almost expecting to find him behind me.

Odd how close to him I felt, when I knew so little about him, as a person. George was but a pale shadow, part of my old belief that a girl grew up, she married, it was expected. And as with any pale shadow that never truly existed, even the memory was fading. A tall man on a rainy night occupied my dreams entirely. My thoughts prowled farther— could it possibly have been Stephen alighting from the train that same rainy night of my arrival? Of course not, I chided myself. Had it been Stephen he would surely have joined us for at least as far as he intended to go. No, it definitely was not Stephen, rather some woodsman, perhaps—there must be those around. Stephen himself traveled about evaluating timber for logging companies, he'd told me.

I straightened at last and rubbed the back of my neck tiredly. I'd been at it for hours and deserved a break; fresh air might help. I'd earlier noted the second exit at the end of the room. Puzzled, I moved the chair blocking it, fully expecting the door to be locked, but it opened at my touch. A long dim passageway stretched before me, with daylight showing farther on. How strange, I thought. Was this one of the escape routes? But whatever the hall's original use, it was now a most amazing repository for books! Both sides were lined with narrow niches, and each niche was heaped with them. The light was poor, and it was impossible to make out the titles, but I suspected this to be an overflow from the library proper, with the second door at the far end opened for ventilation. And I was right I saw, as I stepped through it; someone, probably Jason, making a point of airing this dank tunnel, since a stone of considerable size had been placed so as to keep the door from swinging shut.

Late-day shadows had already gathered as I made my way by a narrow, weedy path through encroaching shrubbery. I found myself in a broad side yard, an area of Montroth's grounds strange to me. There was some evidence of it once having been a formal garden, with the remains of a summerhouse, and benches scattered here and there, some of them almost overgrown with native brush. It had all gone to seed now. The benches were weathered, the roof of the summerhouse caved in, the raveled remnants of birds' nests swinging forlornly in the gnarled branches of untrimmed trees.

But the sun was setting, and though the corridors of surrounding timber were dark, sunset's ruddy glow touched the tops of the evergreens with a fairy brush. I was captivated, so completely engrossed I failed at first to hear my name spoken in a low voice behind me.

I swung to confront the tall figure, and was conscious of the great leap of joy my heart felt. Stephen Landrau! He wore no hat, and a lock of raven hair fell over his forehead. I stared at his deep gray eyes, so dark as to be almost black, and the same strong jaw and straight lips I remembered. Tension seemed to crackle in the air for one endless moment as we faced each other without speaking.

His searching gaze went over me carefully, minutely, then returned to my face. He seemed to relax and there was the hint of a grin. "I was afraid of frightening you, coming upon you so suddenly like this. Of course I could have gone around to the front, knocked on the door and announced myself properly. But I saw you as I came up."

I found my voice. "I don't think I was frightened," I said truthfully, "maybe startled. It isn't every day that—well, someone drops in."

He looked around and shook his head. "I can believe it. A bit off the beaten track, you might say. I've never been this far north before. This must be one of the finest stands of fir in the province."

Naturally he would notice that; it was his job to notice such things. We'd been walking and came to a bench deeply screened by shrubbery where we sat down.

"Miles and miles of it," I agreed. "I felt intimidated when I first came."

"And now?"

"I'm getting used to it and really don't mind at all."

"Then you don't find it lonely."

"N-no. I work in the library, you see, cataloguing books, and it keeps me as busy as I want to be. And then there is this huge house."

"Huge, yes." He took his time surveying it, then smiled down at me. "Obviously English—somewhat English."

I felt my own lips curve in a smile. "It is, with individual overtones. But old. You see the gardens, everything falling down or covered with moss. Inside, all the rooms give the feeling of age too, locked in the past."

"A brave relic. The owners—your aunts—showed courage carving an empire out of the wilderness." Again he tipped his head to study the house, clearly appreciative. He must like old places, that was why he was so interested in this one. I hadn't seen his horse, but perhaps, preferring to walk, he'd left the animal tethered in the trees down the road. I'd have liked very much to ask him in and thought he would be wondering why I'd not done so, but with Aunt Mellie's acid tongue and the aunts' resistance to strangers, I didn't dare. When he said he hadn't long, that he was on his way to a point east of here and had stopped off at Montroth, I didn't know whether to be relieved or sorry. "Have you been back to Vancouver since you left?"

I shook my head. "No. It's so far, and I wouldn't want to leave them that long. The handyman only goes out every two or three months."

"And nobody comes this way much."

"Well—rarely. There have been a few over the years, but my aunts enjoy their isolation."

"Help would be pretty hard to get, this far out," he suggested. "They're not bedridden, I hope."

"Oh no. But maybe not in too stable health, either. Aunt Lollie is the one that worries me. She is prone to what she terms 'upsets'; fortunately, they never seem to last long. So far the other aunt, Aunt Mellie, has remained quite well."

There was a pause. A sudden, sharp gust of wind shook the leaves of the shrubbery behind us; some large black bird hovered briefly over us, like a bad omen, then swooped up over the house and was gone. All too swiftly, daylight had faded, the brightness vanishing from the tops of the trees.

"Cold?"

"No. Only sometimes—it's nothing, really," I said, "nothing at all. Was that thunder I heard?"

"A rumble, yes. When it's warm like this it can happen. They have some big storms in this part of the country," Stephen said with a forcefulness I'd not heard before. "Unpredictable. I hate to think of—I suppose I shouldn't say it, but I can't believe this is a very easy life for you. Would you consider leaving?"

"Oh, I couldn't," I said quickly. "I'm the only family they have left, and they need me."

He nodded. "So that's the way. And I overstepped my bounds. Forget I said it."

"No," I protested, and had the urge to reach and touch him. "No, it's not that at all. But you see how it is—" I gestured, "this gloomy old place, no one but themselves—"

"And you're young and strong and can help. Just don't let the sunshine go from your smile."

I took a deep breath. The chill was all gone, the gloom, and I felt free and good again as I'd felt before. We talked, then, of other things, of ourselves, exchanging details of our lives. He was the second of four brothers, born in Montreal, but had emigrated to the United States. One brother was in the Orient, another was reading law in New York, the third with a large ranch in the southern United States. He, Stephen, liked the outdoors and made regular pilgrimages to visit his parents, who still lived in Montreal.

"Now I want to know about you, all about you."

"What about me? Nothing spectacular." I briefly sketched my childhood, my father, the home in Sussex sold after his death, coming here.

When he stood up at last he drew me with him. I'd looked at his hands, broad and strong across the knuckles, a man radiating strength and purpose. I felt that strength now, and some tremendous power that drew me.

His gaze held mine, it was like a caress. Words, commonplace words, had fallen like snowflakes between us, but in this moment I knew what he meant to say, before he said it.

"I wanted to see you. I couldn't get you out of my mind. When I left you standing there in the rain, with the rain on your face—It wouldn't have made any difference how far, I had to come."

I heard my voice, barely above a whisper. "I'm so glad you did."

He raised my hand to his lips, pressed a kiss into the palm and folded my fingers gently over it. "Keep it safe," he said.

I watched him go, blinking the mist from my eyes, then finally turned back to the house. There should be nothing secret about his visits, nothing clandestine, and next time I was determined he would be properly presented. After all this was not the Dark Ages, and the aunts would understand and welcome him.

By now daylight was almost fully gone. It could be later than I thought and tardiness would invite a barrage of questions, or worse. I let myself in through the side door and in doing so, met Belinda. "Wow, are you going to get it," she quipped, then at my startled look added, "No, I was only teasing." She laughed, shaking her curls, her eyes dancing with mischief, as if she knew something I didn't know and was enjoying it hugely. "Dinner won't be served for another hour yet, so you're safe."

I nodded with relief and in the library, by lamplight, went back to sorting books. For a while it was difficult to concentrate. Stephen—the essence of him, the feel of him—was with me.

The door leading outside was closed. Curious, I carried the lamp into the narrow hall and lifting the light, scanned the tumbled volumes. Here were riches more impressive than any I had so far seen. Dickens, Poe—there was a great set of Poe, very nearly, I thought, everything he ever wrote. Works dealing with murder were much in evidence, even more of them here than in the outer room. The list of grisly tales seemed endless. Each such volume was heavily marked on its flyleaf, *M.M.*, a precaution wholly unnecessary, I was sure, for Aunt Lollie's preferences ran in different channels. Here were romances, vast numbers of them, love in various stages all the way from Greek and Roman days to the present, or at least up to the time the aunts had left England.

But this collection would take more careful perusal, and the light was still inadequate. There was a larger lamp—I'd seen it on the table—but I didn't want to bother to light it now, so returned to the outer room.

I looked up as Aunt Mellie came in. She peered over my shoulder and clucked in satisfaction. "Nice, nice," she exclaimed. "Such a bustling little English girl! But I told you, you need not jump into this so hard. Take your time. I did mention, didn't I, that I am writing my memoirs? One day soon we will get together and you can take notes."

Before I could recover from my surprise, she left with a cheery wave of her hand. When she'd spoken of the memoirs before, she'd been extremely negative. And the terrible scolding, the fury at my tumble into the cellar? All past history, apparently. I'd never seen her this way, not in a mood of such excessive good will, and somehow I distrusted it.

Where had Stephen gone after departing Montroth? To a point east of here, was all he said. It was so vague. There were many things I'd have liked to tell him, to discuss, but the time hadn't seemed right. I'd have liked very much to know what he thought about the note, for instance. After the initial shock when I'd read the warning, I had ceased to be really frightened, but who sent it and why did nag at me. No danger had evolved and I could almost convince myself it was a prank. But for what reason? And if it was a serious threat, who would want me out of here?

Once I'd caught Hessit watching me fixedly and was sure the woman wanted to say something, but she turned her back and walked away quickly, and I was once again left with my doubts. I'd found myself even suspecting the cook—a farfetched notion; Narcisse, mountainous, brawny, with the tread of an elephant, sneaking around halls? Actually I didn't think Narcisse liked me very well. The one time I'd been to the kitchens since literally falling on my knees before her, she'd done a fine job of ignoring me. Nor had Ana acknowledged my presence, though I knew she was aware of me. No, I could definitely rule out Narcisse. That left Belinda, Ana, or Hessit. Belinda was out, and Ana? No, not Ana either. Her world was the kitchen. She'd not venture into the main house, and never the upstairs. I wondered about Hessit, but always came back to the same question—Why?

The evening meal was without incident; once again, the gleaming silver and crystal were used. This time, across the long expanse, I faced my Aunt Lollie instead of Aunt Mellie.

"Does she often remain away from table at mealtime?" I asked.

Aunt Lollie fluttered her little hands. "Oh my no, not often, only occasionally when she wishes to do so. No doubt Hessit has taken a tray up to her."

"Then is she well? I mean, there's nothing wrong?"

"No. She is well. Do not worry about her. Sister is quite capable of taking care of herself." Aunt eyed me, smiling.

"Do enjoy your soufflé, dear. When you have finished I have a surprise for you."

I looked at this little creature, all atwitter in her ruffles and bows, and felt warmth wash over me. Rings and heady scent—heliotrope, of course—and the gigantic pile of twists, swirls and rolls upon her head. By contrast, Aunt Mellie allowed herself only two corkscrew curls above each ear, the remainder of the hair drawn up tightly and skewered with tortoiseshell pins.

Aunt Lollie touched her lips daintily with a napkin, then pushed back her chair. "Now if you are ready—"

What was it? Cards? Table-tipping? The fact that I'd told her I knew nothing of such things, would make no difference. I was fairly certain what she wanted. Reluctantly I followed her upstairs.

Aunt's suite was on the floor above my own. When she unlocked the door and it swung open, I reeled back, gasping. The atmosphere was stifling with perfumed heat, and as soon as I was able to catch my breath and step inside, I found myself faced with the most exaggerated opulence I'd ever seen. Prominently displayed in one corner of the room against a backdrop of heavy black velvet were the trappings of Aunt Lollie's prime interest—the inducements to her "companions." Crystal ball on a silver tray, ear trumpets, vials of some volatile fluid, smaller crystal globes and glass bottles of varying sizes, and a Planchette, were all arranged on a velvet-draped table of inlaid mother-of-pearl.

In another corner of the room was a dressing table laden with innumerable jars and boxes of powders, lotions, creams and perfumes, and mirrors of all conceivable shapes and sizes; one mirror was full-length and very nearly as wide, strategically placed so a little old lady might admire herself to her heart's content.

The long curtains at the windows were of heavy lavender satin, faded but still impressive, the bed canopy deeply frilled and of the same shade, with satin ribbon bows at each corner. The rug underfoot was threadbare Turkish, while the remainder of the furniture, bed tables, bedstead, ottoman, chairs, stools, were all of some dark wood, lavender-upholstered and richly carved. Even the fireplace was pink-veined Italian marble, with gigantic portraits in gilt frames of the members of the royal family on either side of it. But which royal family?

"God save the King," Aunt Lollie murmured unctuously and I flinched. She'd been jostled back in time, but this far back? She'd forgotten, of course. An incredibly callow William gazed down at me; a youth, I thought, all of fourteen, flanking him baby Albert, Duke of Clarence. The other portraits were of the Duchess of Kent and her husband the Duke. There was no likeness in evidence of Victoria, reigning queen of England.

Little Aunt Lollie was standing with hands clasped, waiting for my approval. "Lovely," I managed. "All of it—just lovely. But don't you think you might—that is—England doesn't have a king any more."

"Doesn't have a—" I'd shocked Aunt Letitia right out of her lace fichu. "My dear, my dear," the old lady babbled, "what *do* we have?"

I explained. It was taking stick-candy from a baby and offering something of lesser value in return. I wasn't at all sure Aunt Lollie could accept it; in the blink of an eye the whole course of English history had been altered for her, and she was scrambling to keep up. She gazed at the portraits pitifully.

"I don't know what I'm going to do with them," she wailed. "And the frames are so pretty, too! Does my sister know about this?" She leaned against my shoulder, dabbing at her eyes. I comforted her, feeling like a criminal. "No, of course not. How could she know? We have no newspapers and no magazines, no news at all. I suppose it is the price one pays for seclusion. We live happily in our world, but sometimes I wonder if others don't continue to move on while we are left standing still. Mind you, we have not missed it! It is only at times like these . . . Ah, well, thank you for telling me. Now we should do what you came to do."

She pulled aside a curtain to reveal a table set with dainty china and fresh apples and cheese in the European fashion. We pulled out chairs, sat down. We'd had no dessert at dinner, but apples? I expressed amazement. Aunt Lollie only nodded.

"Oh, we have a fine orchard out back!" A pained look crossed her face and was as suddenly gone, leaving her smiling and mischievous. "And have Jason show you the blueberry patch sometime—my sister is having trouble with her blueberries."

I hadn't seen any blueberries, but something else puzzled me. "A lot of strange things have happened, and one of the strangest is what I found when I fell into that cellar. B-r-r! Kegs, jugs and shoes. Why would anyone want to keep old shoes? I've never seen that many lined up in anybody's storehouse!"

"Sh—!" Aunt Lollie's little hand flew to cover her mouth. "*Shoes?* But my dear, I don't—" Some intelligence came to her and turned her sly. "Old objects do collect," she observed mildly, "and we've lived here a long time. I doubt my sister even knew they were there—she just hates to destroy anything which might be of use. One cannot realize how such throwaways do pile up. You found furniture too, didn't you?"

"Among other things," I agreed grimly and glanced up to meet the old lady's pointed stare. "Rats by the dozen, I mean. At least it seemed like dozens."

"Oh. Oh! Yes. Nasty things, aren't they? We must have Jason clear them out. More apples, dear? More cheese?" I shook my head, she rose, sweetly smiling, and pointed to the black-draped table. "I saw you looking at my Cozy Corner. Sometime I want you to try my little friend Planchette. I know it is very late, almost eight o'clock and past bedtime so we cannot get into it tonight, but soon?"

I gave an evasive answer and escaped. A Cozy Corner? I'd sidestep that as long as I could. Somewhat bewildered, I returned to my room. As soon as I opened the door I stood stock-still, rooted to the spot and unable to believe my eyes. The place had not only been ransacked, it looked as if a cyclone had ripped through it. Someone had entered my suite and my clothing was wildly strewn about, a lamp overturned. Automatically I picked up the lamp and replaced it on the table; the shade was broken, the kerosene spilled. My reticule was on the bed and the Vancouver paper had gone. The note, too, was gone, the dresser cover askew, my coat lying half on a chair, half on the floor, a scarf making a blue puddle on the rug beside it. I reached for the scarf and again halted. I yearned to pitch into the disordered bed and, frankly, have a tantrum. Who could derive pleasure from such a deed? It was sheer maliciousness—it had to be. I'd forgotten to lock my door and this, then, was the result.

↶ 6 ↷

MY FIRST THOUGHT was to go to Aunt Mellie
and let her take care of it. She would know how to handle
unauthorized entries. But what could she do? Question
everyone? Undoubtedly lose her temper, which was never
too stable anyway. I should be able to figure out some
things for myself.

I put the suite to rights, thinking hard. It didn't matter about the newspaper, that had probably gone into a
wastebasket long since. I hadn't kept track of it. But the
note was something else. I'd known where that was; I'd
seen it only yesterday. Had someone other than the sender
known of it and for some reason determined to get it? No,
that didn't make sense. And if the sender wanted the note
back, there'd been no need for such upheaval; on the other
hand, this could be the work of someone else, someone
bent upon sheer mischief. Or suppose there had been *two*
people, one after the note and the other intending only
destruction? But who of all these persons I knew would do
such a thing? No, that didn't make sense either. Somehow
I'd erred, gotten off the track.

At midnight, with the rooms once more in order, I sank
wearily into the tub to soak, reveling in the hot water but
sparing with the soap—homemade, yellow, hard, and very,
very harsh. I'd already learned a little went a long way.

Toweling off briskly a short while later, my eye caught
a flash of red, a tiny scrap of yarn clinging to a sliver of the
door casing. I reached out and pulled it off carefully. Where

60

had I seen this particular shade of red before? I looked again at the small shred of yarn and comprehension came slowly to me. Ana. And I'd thought she wouldn't venture into the main house, and certainly not upstairs! As for the note and what became of it, I was reasonably sure I could settle that, too.

I picked up my father's portrait and studied it. The features were so familiar, so dear. Good night, Daddy, I murmured. If you'd lived you never would have believed this. Would you have pondered upon the slow twilight of these aristocrats and had the patience I can never muster? He was the kindest person I'd ever known. Miss him? I would always miss him. But tears were for then, this was now. I squared my shoulders, placing the picture again on the table at my bedside.

On impulse, I blew out the lamp and pulled a chair up to the window, leaning my arms on the sill to look out. The front of the house and the shrubbery at its corners cast long shadows in the soft moonlight. Some winged creature—a bird or a bat—cut a swift pattern across the night sky and vanished. Another bird echoed his plaintive cry deep in the timber.

There was something the matter with this household, and I didn't know what. I'd gone back to the cellar to look for my locket, lost, I thought, in my struggle to escape, and found it, chain broken, between the steps and the wall. Entry had not been difficult; I'd simply waited until Narcisse stepped on to the back porch, then pulled open the huge door. The weird odor had dissipated. Light from matches showed a floor clean-swept of glass, jugs and jars removed, shoes and clothing gone. Only the barrels remained lined against the walls. But there was something unholy about the place, something dank and forbidding, and I couldn't get out fast enough.

More and more too, I wondered about the quality of help employed at Montroth. Jason, impaired; Ana—I didn't know about Ana. I'd met Haines, a kindly, stooped old man

who, like Jason, was unable to speak. Hessit, I knew by
now, was also mute. And the dogs, far from being vicious,
rushed to the fence to lick my hands. Aunt Mellie's terror
was her own, I could find no reason for it.

My thoughts swerved as the quiet of the night fell completely upon me, blotting out all warmth. I shivered, though
I did not know why. Some prickling sixth sense, some
premonition of danger, reached out and gripped me, the
foreboding I'd felt so strongly on first entering the house
was with me once again.

I knew I should go to bed, but still I lingered, and
suddenly started, leaning forward, staring below. A figure
had broken from the shadows and moved across a patch of
bright moonlight. It was crouched and dragging something.
Was it an animal? A dog? No, hunched over, it still walked
upright on its feet. Hooded and caped in some dark fabric,
the figure paused beneath my window and looked upward,
then faded into the deeper shadows at the corner of the
house.

Had it seen me? My heart was in my throat, my mouth
absolutely dry. It wasn't Jason, the creature was too slight
for that, yet with strength sufficient to drag its burden.
Almost at once the dogs erupted in frenzy.

Who was it? It had been too far away and the face under
the cowl too well hidden for any possible identification. But
I was sure it was not Haines, not Narcisse, not Hessit. Hessit
was not small and bent.

I got into bed where I lay stiff and questioning. I clutched
for my common sense, and finally succeeded in calming
myself somewhat.

In a gorgeous walnut fourposter under a toasty eiderdown
quilt, I'd sleep to the tune of howling dogs and the calming
clank of the boiler in the bathroom. Outside was the mystery
of night, but inside it was warm and cozy with the last of
the firelight flickering against the walls. The room was
the same, the brass hod on the hearth freshly loaded with
sweet-smelling wood knots, the brass-bound bellows beside

it. Hessit, as she always did, had stoked the fire carefully. Hessit, neither young nor old, who merely glided, who came and went soundlessly, the faithful servant; I was certain, now, that she was the answer to one of the problems.

The first thing I did upon arising the next morning was to fly to the window and look down. Nothing, of course. What had I expected to see? Long rays of bright sunshine threaded the treetops to lie in golden bars across the road, and the early morning air was clean and fresh and fine. Spring would always be a latecomer here, but was out in full force today.

The water in the pitcher was biting cold—the boiler heated but once a day—and I hurried to ready myself. I remained in my room until Hessit arrived with fresh linens. She knocked lightly and I bid her to enter. I said nothing until she completed her tasks and was ready to leave. When she turned with the laundry in her arms I spoke.

"Hessit," I said quietly, "I want to thank you for your warning, but I'm all right. I'll *be* all right. Do you hear? Nothing is going to happen. What could? There is no danger, none whatsoever. I don't know what danger you could have meant, anyway. What are *you* afraid of?"

The woman turned to flee but I barred the way. "No— wait! I want to find out something. First, how many keys are there to my rooms? Three? Two? Two, and I have one. No one else has a key to this suite besides yourself? Fine."

As if she knew what was coming, Hessit began to shake her head; her mouth opened but no sound came. Again she commenced backing away, again I signaled her to remain. "Please! I'm not going to hurt you. I only want to talk. Now, I know you have to get in to do the rooms, but someone else was in this suite last night. I forgot and left the door unlocked. You see? When I came back the place was a mess, everything torn apart. Then I saw the note was gone—the note, you understand? It was gone. That's the most important thing. You wrote that note, did you take it back?"

The Jamaican woman's dark face convulsed. She seemed about to speak but could not, tears standing in her eyes with the force of her emotions. Words gurgled in her throat. She dropped her linens and flung her hands wide. She was speaking urgently, rapidly with her hands, her shoulders; yes, she had taken it and destroyed it. She was afraid. She would not tell why! There—right there was where she found it, on the dressing table under the cover. She had looked for the note and found it. The room was good then, everything all right. She hadn't done it. Did I blame her?

"No." I shook my head. No, I knew Hessit wasn't responsible for that. But why a warning in the first place?

The woman's body began to tremble, and she glanced over her shoulder and shook her head violently; I had never seen sheer terror so strongly mirrored upon a human face. She tried to tell me she had to go now. She had to leave. Her eyes, grown huge, pleaded with me to understand. I understood, all right. Wasn't Hessit Jamaican, from a hot lush land where taboos could still rule the minds and lives of its people? Hessit was shaken half out of her wits with unreasoning horror by some shadow from her past, a lingering superstition which yet held her in its thrall. What this had to do with a warning, or why she felt it could affect me, I didn't know. Nor, I saw, was I about to find out. She had reached her limits and there was nothing to be gained by further questioning. Faced with such fear, I had to be gentle.

"I'm sorry." I smiled, trying to make the gesture reach across to still her agitation. "I didn't mean to frighten you so. I won't ask any more questions and you can go now, if you like." Hessit gave me a pleading look, snatched up her laundry, and fled. It wasn't the full answer I'd hoped for, but it would have to do. I descended to the library, moved the chair and found the tunnel with its niches of jumbled books already open. I quickly walked through it and emerged into the bright sunshine. Taking the route I'd taken before, I found the bench where Stephen and I had sat and here paused, my desires once more upon me. Then I shook myself and continued on. Picking my way carefully, I blazed a new path around grass clumps and through tangles of weeds to the front of the house and the drive, to search for signs of last night's activity.

But there were no tracks; there was no indication of anything having been dragged. Puzzled, I retraced my steps to my starting point, replaced the chair and, finding no one around, headed for the lower regions. Belinda seemed to have a pretty good grasp of what went on at Montroth. I'd talk to her.

I reckoned without Aunt Mellie. "Where are you going?" she demanded. "Come, I have everything ready."

The memoirs, of course. I'd been forced to sit through endless recitals of the deeds of illustrious forebears; the memoirs, no doubt, would take up where they left off. I reminded myself that I had offered to help.

In the big drawing room a table had been pulled forward, pencils and paper placed upon it, and without further delay we got down to business. We worked our way through two hours of family history "from dear Papa's branch of the Montroths, before he married Mama." Lunchtime came and went with no letup in the task at hand.

Still later, at a lull in the tale, I put in, "You did mention that you'd been working on this, didn't you? How much do you have completed, other than what we have here, I mean? I'd love to see it, if it's handy."

Aunt Mellie viewed me as if from a great distance, a vast, cold distance. "Do not hurry me. I suppose you are used to a life that is all rush, rush, rush. Well, it is different at Montroth. As to the other section of the work, all in good season. In the meantime if I choose to keep you here taking notes or merely listening, that is my affair."

All so quickly had Aunt slipped into one of her brittle moods; I realized my error and tried to step around it. "Very well. Do you want to continue now?"

Unexpectedly, Aunt Mellie smiled. "I realize sometimes I must be an old bear. Please forgive me. I shall try, in future, to act more pleasantly."

The moment was too much for me; on impulse, I leaned forward and swiftly bestowed a kiss on her withered cheek, which she brushed at furiously.

"That is not necessary! I am not given to vulgar displays, so do not do it again! Mawkish sentimentality has never appealed to me. Now where were we? Oh yes, you were asking if we should continue. I think not, not right now at any rate. But do keep yourself available. I shall need you quite regularly from now on. You can get back to the library later. There is plenty of time."

I wanted to ask her about the books in the hallway, but I didn't. I wondered if I should tell her about Stephen, but discarded the idea at once. Her moods were so mercurial I couldn't risk it. Not now, anyway.

"Sometimes I wonder if you are who you say you are," she was saying. "You don't favor your father, at least not since you've grown up."

"I've been told I look like my mother."

"Humph. You don't act like a sheltered girl, either. So self-confident—very sturdy. His death didn't bother you at all, did it?"

"Very much!"

Aunt searched my face avidly. "But I don't see you sorrowing. It was not too long ago, was it? After all, one can expect— You don't mope about, carry on. That is unusual in one so young. You obviously have your emotions in good check."

"I don't cry," I said slowly, "if that's what you mean. I almost never cry. I thought the world would end when he went, and waited for it to do so. But nothing happened. Life went on as before. I sold the house; I came here. And that's all there is to it."

Again she smiled, nodding. "You're direct, too. I like you! As a matter of fact if I hadn't, you'd have— Ah, well, never mind. You're cheeky it's true, but also have fortitude. I will say in all honesty that I would wish my daughter— had I had one!—to be like you."

"Why, that's nice. Very nice." I was warmed and pleased. It was a rare compliment. Aunt Lollie showed her feelings readily, for this aunt warmth seemed difficult, and so much jealousy existed between them.

"My sister is a simpering fool," Aunt Mellie stated grimly, almost as if she had read my thoughts. "You are not to believe a thing she says. She has lapses of memory, is criminally accusatory at times, and most irksome to get along with. Of later years she has become impossible! She is covetous, vain and irresponsible in her actions—she has always been that. I never could understand what men saw in her. Twittering, affecting her scents and bonbons, her silks and laces. I find it disgusting!"

Which provided a little enlightenment I decided, but was diplomatically silent. I picked up the pad and the notes I had been taking and said, "I have it all down," indicating paragraphs of names and corresponding dates. "I can put them in order right away if you like."

There was no reply. Fortunately Hessit arrived then with the steaming pot, scones, marmalade and the most delicious shortbread I had ever eaten. Again I tendered a mental accolade to the artisan who could concoct such miracles.

"I notice," I suggested when the woman had gone, "that Hessit never says anything. Is it some speech impediment, perhaps?"

"She has had her tongue cut out," Aunt Mellie said mildly, and I dropped my scone. "She's Jamaican, from one of the interior tribes where voodoo is still practiced. She violated one of their taboos as a girl."

My scalp prickled. I'd known there was some reason she couldn't speak, but not this. Aunt had recounted the details in the most casual fashion—of course it was a long time ago, I told myself shakily, she had had plenty of time to have become used to the idea.

"I'm sorry," I managed, "I didn't know."

"No, of course not." Aunt Mellie pulled the fragile china cups forward and helped herself to tea, then poured for me. "And Jason. He was born incapacitated. He couldn't speak, only babbled. Then at thirteen he fell from a horse, broke his back and both legs. He recovered and was able to live a normal life up to a point. He was with us in England, a gardener to the family. He still serves occasionally in that capacity. We have kept him on because—well, he has nowhere else to go. And he does raise the finest rhododendrons. You may have noticed. The soil here seems particularly suited to them. I love rhododendrons, don't you? Jason's hearing began to fail in later years—he is all of eighty, you understand."

"He doesn't look it!"

"Most assuredly not. He lives a very sheltered life, and we see to it that his duties are not strenuous, though he is most dreadfully strong in those arms of his. It is said he once killed a man, simply crushed him to death. I should hate to see such strength fully exerted! I imagine once those arms were wrapped around a victim, the victim would soon suffocate. And Jason is very devoted. He would protect us—me—with his life."

"Yes, one can see he is very devoted." Yet again, I reserved judgment. I couldn't imagine anyone with the sweet gentle smile of a child and the manners of a courtly gentleman squeezing anybody in his grasp.

"The dogs didn't bother you last night?" she asked.

"Not too much."

"One night in ten," Aunt muttered. "Mr. Owens—Harold, brought the abominable creatures with him when he came. Before a fence could be built two of them ran off into the forest and were killed. At least they never returned." As for Mr. Owens, Aunt Mellie added, he was actually a friend of a friend who had decided to look them up. He couldn't stay as long as they wished and they missed him terribly when he left. He was such an active person, always doing something.

I seemed to recall Belinda had mentioned a Mr. Owens. But this fear of the dogs was even worse than Belinda had said. Maybe in the months ahead I could help her overcome it. I set down my cup.

"More tea?"

"No, thanks. I have loved this little talk, the chance to be together and chat."

But Aunt had suddenly impaled me with a hard stare. "You don't remember it, do you? I dislike liars."

"Don't remember—" I thought fast, trying to follow her. "Oh, you mean the house. Only as much as I said. And as I said, I was young then—"

"Three when we remodeled. Five the last time you saw it, before your father ran off to Australia on that wild goose chase."

"It was his job! He had to go, his firm sent him."

"And then his firm went bankrupt! I do not consider that a wise venture, and if I recall, I said as much at the time."

"He wasn't gone long," I attempted to explain, "only a year for the work he had to do. He came back as soon as he could. It was while we were away that Aunt Lollie was hurt, wasn't she, in that—"

"Not hurt!" Aunt bit off the words. "We had competent doctors examine her. Your father knew that!"

I wondered if she had brought up the subject again only to blame my father. Useless to point out to Aunt that she was wrong, that I was nine, not five as she had suggested. But nine or five, what was the difference? The time was long past, and whether I remembered the house or not, or how much of it, must be immaterial.

It was a wearing day, and it seemed that Aunt had gone out of her way to be difficult. I would have liked to escape outdoors, as had become my habit whenever I could, but it was late, already dinner time—a quiet meal, for I ate it entirely alone.

My strong curiosity demanded to know about the figure that had prowled last night, and once again I turned to the kitchens. Belinda, on the porch folding linens from a basket, straightened and waggled a finger. "Hi! Come on and sit— I've got a minute. Be dark pretty soon but there's a while. Twilight's pretty, isn't it? Doesn't last long up here in the trees, though. You look worried. What's the matter?" She dropped to the steps, and I sat down beside her.

"Oh, nothing, really." I hesitated, feeling somewhat foolish at telling a tale that sounded like the far stretch of imagination. "Well, I guess there is, too. At least I'm ready to agree with you—the place is spooky. You should have seen what I saw last night." I shuddered, I couldn't help myself. "Somebody dressed all in black and crouched over, dragging something. And wait—you haven't heard everything yet. It stopped right under my window and looked up. I'm not easily frightened—at least I hadn't thought so, but I admit I was absolutely petrified."

She had been listening intently, and now to my amazement, burst into laughter. "That was me—that was me! Did I scare you? I'm sorry. I was wearing that same darned shroud I used making candles so the pitch from the knots wouldn't get on my clothes."

I was stunned. "In the middle of the night?"

"Sure!" She grinned. "I'd forgotten to do it before and Narcisse cracked the whip. No wood to cook with, no cooking. I used a gunny bag to haul 'em so I wouldn't have to make so many trips. Haven't you noticed that pile Jason brought up? That's where they came from, only I took a shortcut."

I drew a deep breath, incredibly relieved. "And it was you looking up at my window? Why didn't you call out?"

Belinda's eyes danced. "I was about to. There you were, stuck in the house, and I was dragging knots for breakfast fires. I figured you should be out having fun, too."

She said she'd seen Stephen the night he came, and liked him. He was nice, very handsome, and I'd made a good choice, she thought. She'd intended to keep their meeting secret, except after my scare, I deserved to know.

He'd asked where to find me but hadn't said much of anything else.

I wanted to ask about the little scullery girl. "Ana—" I said. "Is she—"

Belinda shrugged. "Not all she should be. She's had a rough time."

Once Ana had peered at me from beneath her brows and offered a shy smile. What would she do the next time I saw her? Her hair was worn as usual, down her back with a twist of red wool at the end of the braid.

"But who is she? Where is she from?"

"Oh, on one of his trips out for staples, Jason just found her wandering around, no place to go, no folks, and brought her home with him. Miss Millicent wasn't very pleased to have an orphan foisted on her, but she put her to work, and I guess Ana's doing all right. At least here, she eats. Still afraid of her own shadow, though. Sometimes she gets a notion in her head and you can't budge it."

"Like what?"

"Well, about the orchard. She'll go any place but there."

"There's nothing wrong with the orchard. She's probably just seen some animal, or heard one back in the woods."

"Maybe." Belinda shrugged again. "I guess I better tell you," she said. "I've given notice."

I was shocked. Belinda—going away? I couldn't imagine Montroth without her. "Do they think I take up too much of your time?"

"Oh no, nothing like that." She explained her mother had been ailing for years, and Belinda thought it best—

At the time I didn't see any loopholes in the explanation; I only knew Belinda was leaving, and how much I'd miss her.

ᏒᎲ 7 ᎡᏮ

THE SISTERS RARELY CONFRONTED one another if they could help it, and when they did meet at table as they were bound to do, both maintained daggers-drawn, icy silence.

These times, aware of the thinness of that ice, I addressed myself strictly to my food, desirous only of finishing the meal and getting away as quickly as I could.

Tonight Aunt Mellie began it. She was particularly goading, and I wondered just how long Aunt Lollie would take it without retaliation.

Hessit served, soft-footed as usual, but I caught the look of apprehension in the woman's eyes, and knew pity. Probably there had been this sort of situation in plenty during the years she had been with the Montroths.

"I noticed you going over your photographs again today," Aunt Mellie said in a jibing tone. Then suddenly her expression altered and she laughed heartily. "Remember Bernie?" she asked and peered at Aunt Lollie for a reaction. "I always say if a man can't learn his trade properly, he's a misfit and shouldn't be allowed to deceive people. He deserved what he got. Isn't that what you say? A liar pays for his lies. Do you recall those hedges? Shocking!"

Aunt Lollie nodded her little head and sighed reminiscently. "Ah, but that was a long time ago. The springtime of innocence."

"Innocence!" Aunt Mellie snapped. "I wouldn't try to appear so lily-white, not with your sins."

"With your sanction!" Aunt Lollie shot back. "And D.J. What about D.J.?"

"Don't try to draw me into that one! It was your planning from the start. Oh, you've been hand-in-glove right along with me. You plan, I execute. We make a great team, don't we, Sister?"

None of this made sense to me. For a brief hopeful moment I'd thought the two were on the same side, their differences patched up, then they were hurling insults at one another again. And little Aunt Lollie, I saw with surprise, was in complete command. Insults or no, it was Aunt Lollie who kept her head and steered the argument the way she wanted it to go.

"*You* sent him back to India," Aunt Mellie cackled shrilly. "That was your idea. But what about the other one? Didn't I—" She broke off and looked at me as if suddenly becoming aware of my presence. For a moment the silence was broken only by the clink of silver on china. I squirmed in my seat. If I could get away—good heavens, one felt like a fifth wheel at these stupid squabbles! But there was more to come, and my heart sank. Aunt Lollie poked daintily at a piece of braised liver on her plate. "I believe you were saying something about photographs, weren't you?"

"Yes!" Aunt Mellie took the bait and plunged headlong. "Did you see any in there of me? I've asked for them back a dozen times. I tell you, I mean to have my pictures!"

Aunt Lollie looked smug. If anybody had her little claws set for battle tonight, I thought, it was Aunt Lollie. She said in a purring tone, "You have mentioned it before and I have told you before. Sister, you've grown senile. Unbelievably absentminded! You forget I gave you yours a long time ago, when you first asked for them—there were only two. What you've done with them since I wouldn't know, surely it's no concern of mine, but don't come back at me again demanding them. Or is it that you simply do not choose to remember?

"Either way you have become extremely boring, so I

will tell you once more—those remaining are mine, and you shan't get them away from me. Now do you understand? They are *mine*."

"I've seen petty thieves before," Aunt Mellie threw back angrily, "but never one quite so brazen! Do you remember that day in London? Walter gave them to me!"

Aunt Lollie's head jerked up; two bright red spots burned on her withered cheeks. She laid down her fork with great care and spoke almost pleasantly. "Next you're going to try to tell me that Walter was in love with you. Why, he hated you, you know, he made fun of you behind your back— laughed and said you were an ugly hussy with your scrawny bones and manlike ways. You had the manners of a wild bull, he said, a bull in a—a china shop. You threw yourself at every man that came to the house—to see *me*."

"Why, you—old—devil!" Aunt Mellie was livid; for a while I thought she was going to hurl her plate at Aunt Lollie. The situation would have been laughable had they not been so utterly serious. Both sisters were in deadly earnest; I thought each of them could have cheerfully killed the other. Hurriedly, I finished my pudding, waiting for an opportunity to leave. One did not depart this table until one or the other of the sisters did so; it was a rule.

Aunt Mellie was panting. "Even that betrothal ring you're wearing is rightfully mine. Don't pretend you don't know it was meant for me! You tricked me, you with your honey ways, and I will hate you for it to my dying day."

"Which, praise heaven, may not be far hence." Little Aunt Lollie's napkin was daintily to her mouth, the words spoken barely loud enough to hear, and I stifled a gasp. A half-emptied glass of blackberry wine stood at Aunt Mellie's elbow, and the old lady pushed it aside. Aunt Lollie sipped hers delicately. She seemed to be waiting for something, patiently waiting, watching Aunt Mellie in a strange catlike way.

Suddenly, furiously, Aunt Mellie seized the glass and drained it, poured another from the decanter and drank that, too. "Your perfume is overpowering—but you always did drench yourself in the stuff. It does nothing for the aged except make them appear ridiculous. Gracious—isn't it hot in here? I feel quite flushed!"

Most happy to seize upon an excuse, I rose quickly. "Would you like me to open a window? Or call Hessit to get you a drink of cold water?"

"Ah," Aunt Lollie murmured with a good deal of satisfaction, "I am finished. I shall summon Hessit myself then go up to my suite. I am quite fatigued. Lorene, you will come to my room later, if you please. I have long awaited our excursion into my Cozy Corner together. And now excuse me, all. Dear Sister, good night."

Aunt Mellie did appear flushed, and her eyes had a glassy look. Abruptly she groaned. "The wine," she gasped, "the wine—" And half rising, she fell over the table in a clatter of dishes. Aunt Lollie had vanished; I jumped forward, calling loudly for Hessit. I thought the old woman was dying—was it some sort of seizure?

Hessit came running, and together we got Aunt upstairs and to bed. By now the old lady was writhing in pain.

"But what's the matter with her?" I cried. "What could have happened? One minute she was sitting talking and the next—" I'd never seen anything like this before. The wine? Yet Aunt Lollie had drunk it too—in fact she'd filled her glass a second time. But Aunt Mellie? Yes, I thought, perhaps she'd had even more.

The old lady's face was gray, her lips colorless, and there were flecks of foam at the corners of her mouth. She looked terrible. She seemed to be struggling to say something, to make herself understood, and presently, between paroxysms, managed to speak.

To me, trying in vain to keep my charge covered, casting hurriedly about for some remedy, the words were shocking in the extreme. "Get out," the old lady shrilled in her reed-thin voice, "both of you! Leave me, I say! Don't just stand there goggling like a pair of idiots, *get out*!"

Was she delirious? I didn't think so, and that made it even worse. I glanced at the Jamaican woman, who shrugged and spread her hands. Had she seen her mistress this way before? Aunt Mellie couldn't be drunk, she hadn't taken enough for that, I was sure. Was there something in the drink that made her deathly sick? That was it. In her rage she'd drunk it off and here she was—as Aunt Lollie, sweet little Aunt Lollie, knew she would be. I turned and left the room. Hessit paused to straighten the coverlet and I heard a crash. The old lady had hurled something at her, some glass object which had struck the door and shattered into splinters on the floor. "Get out," Aunt Mellie screamed, "*get out of here and leave me alone!*"

I'd never been in Aunt Mellie's quarters before and upon entering had had my brief impressions. It was a place stamped with grimness, filled with old rags and dishes saved from who-knew-when. The worn washcloth and towel and the few toilet articles that lay about bespoke of the austerity of her life. I'd felt deep sympathy. But not now! Now I would not have blamed Hessit if she'd slammed the door off the hinges. And what was Aunt Lollie doing now in her satin-upholstered trundle bed—laughing? I looked back down the hall then deliberately turned in the other direction.

There had been flareups of varying intensity before, but this was the worst. Last time they fought it was over meat pie; the time before, Aunt Mellie had sworn her sister stole a box of handkerchiefs. But nothing—nothing had ever been as bad as this.

Anxiety nagged at me. Maybe I shouldn't have left so soon. Suppose Aunt Lollie became ill too? Reluctantly, I climbed the stairs again and knocked on Aunt Lollie's door. I had to knock twice. A choked voice told me to enter. Aunt sat bolt upright in her bed with a lapboard on her knees and playing cards scattered all over the counterpane. Between the walls of the room, the heat and scent and the odor of stagnation lay as heavily as before. Aunt Lollie stared straight ahead, her eyes with the fixed intensity of a sleepwalker, and I knew she saw nothing.

I cried, "Aunt Lollie, are you all right?" and moved forward quickly. My approach roused her; she suddenly flung the board aside and wringing her hands, commenced to weep.

"I played my solitaire," she gabbled, "and all that came up were spades, spades—all spades! They mean death. Nothing like this has happened before! Lorene, what have you done to us? I feel it is the end—death rides on the wind for the last of the Montroths. As we have done to them, so they do to us, all in good time, all in good time—"

I soothed her, got her back into bed, and settled her down. Of all the stupid delusions! I would have preferred arguing the old lady out of her superstitious fears, pointing out their silly absurdity, but instead sat beside her and held her hand until she fell into uneasy sleep.

I looked in on Aunt Mellie again; she lay flat on her back, snoring loudly.

I returned to my room and tried to sleep myself. But although I was tired, there were too many questions arising that I couldn't answer to let me rest. Superstitions, phobias—the past cast long shadows. What had happened to make them this way? Was it the shape of things to come? Or would the dust settle and Montroth be at least no worse than it was before Aunt Mellie thought her sister had tried to poison her. Or was it a seizure brought on by her rage? I didn't know what to think.

The next day, into this household of seethe and ferment, George came. George, my former fiancé, whom I'd thought never to see again! I didn't ask by what means he had arrived, all I could think of was how to get rid of him. There was no way in the world I could present him to the aunts, both barricaded behind their closed doors.

"Greetings, my dear Lorene, my dear, dear Lorene! It is so wonderful to see you at last!" He reached as if to embrace me, but I moved aside. "It is quite a trip up here."

"Yes," was all I could find to say. I'd allowed him into the front hall, and momentum carried me into the drawing room. I waved a hand vaguely, indicating that he should be seated. He gazed at me in the way I remembered. What I hadn't remembered was the disposition to plumpness, the well-fed, well-cosseted look of a pampered son. He drew off his pearl gray gloves and glanced about with ill-concealed curiosity.

My head still in a whirl, I managed conversation as best I could. He obviously planned to stay; one would not travel so far without expecting to do so. I could imagine the House falling down around my ears when his presence became known. More to the point, where would I put him? Better still, how could I get him on his way again. Several alternatives raced through my mind, but I discarded them all. It was best to be honest, straightforward.

"I have two aunts, as you undoubtedly remember, but both are severely incapacitated. I am afraid they can receive no one."

"A pity!" George's round face showed signs of dismay, and I knew exactly what he was thinking. "I should like very much to meet them, though I suppose that is impossible. I gather they are confined to bed."

"Oh, most definitely!"

George sighed. "That is too bad. I've always gotten on well with old people, and hoped to make an impression. Do you foresee prolonged confinement?"

Perched on the edge of my chair, I shrugged lightly. "One cannot tell. Of course at their age—both are in their seventies, you understand—it would be impossible and most indelicate to predict—"

"Oh yes! Naturally. Well, it appears I've come at a bad time. I'll not remain as long as I planned then. But perhaps you can put me up overnight."

It was true he couldn't have come at a worse time. He should not have come at all! After my decisive refusal to marry him and our parting back in England, I failed to see what possible expectations he could still entertain. Undoubtedly it was his mama; I could see her fine hand in this. What her Georgie wanted, Georgie got.

Politeness prompted my inquiry as to her health, though I couldn't have cared either way. It seemed she'd come up with a new proposal—that we marry and live in her house next door. I found this quite as unacceptable as the former suggestion, that we marry and move in with her.

The image of Stephen, tall, broad-shouldered, rose up before me. I looked at this potted little man and wondered how, even in my worst moments, I could have considered marrying him. But he'd come a long way, a very long way, and deserved consideration. I tried to be kind, to be polite.

He stayed four days, the longest days of my life, trailing everywhere I went, fawning over me with compliments until I wanted to scream. I looked lovely, precisely the same, I'd not changed a bit though it had been—how long had it been? All this time Montroth's third floor remained locked in icy silence. Hessit traveled up and down with trays. However funereal this atmosphere must have seemed to George, it failed to dampen his ardor; my declaration on the fourth day did that.

He'd been on my heels going down the hall. "George." I stopped, he very nearly bumped into me. "I will not marry you, I will not move in with your mother, into the house next door to your mother or anywhere else. I am happy here, actually quite content. It is my duty to remain with my aunts and care for them. Nothing you can say will induce me to go back with you. My place is here and I am staying."

He left that same afternoon. Jason drove him, the trap hired to bring him one way to Montroth not so easy to summon at will—this, George had not known.

I watched the coach disappear down the driveway and sighed with relief. That part of my life was over, now, for good. Expecting interrogation, I patiently answered questions; I had to. It was not a pleasant scene. Who was that? the aunts demanded. I explained. Yes, he was gone, and no, he wasn't coming back. I said I'd left no one in England and that was the truth. No, I hadn't invited him! How could I? Nor had I the slightest idea he would come. His appearance was totally unexpected. I knew Aunt Mellie didn't believe me.

Belinda was gone, and I felt at loose ends. But the House was settling back into its more or less even tenor. Daily I catalogued books, and one early morning, with a mission in mind, I slipped away to the kitchens. Much to my surprise, Narcisse welcomed me.

"You breakfast?" she demanded.

I shook my head. "Not yet."

"You eat. Toast? Hotcake? I fix. Lori plenty skinny. Get nice, fat. Round." She shrugged her massive shoulders. "I fix, you eat."

Soon she set apple juice, feathery pancakes, fresh syrup, bacon and steaming coffee before me; this meal was a revelation. Jason appeared briefly at the back door upon some matter of business, and his eyes widened when he saw me. I smiled pleasantly, and after a moment's hesitation he clawed his cap from his grizzled head and answered in kind. This from a man who crushed people? Fiddlesticks, I thought.

Narcisse hovered nearby, eyed me, went, and came again. "You no tell Missy M.?" she blurted suddenly.

"No." I scraped the last of the pancake from my plate.

"Why you no tell? You tell, that girl get in bad trouble." She laid a brooch on the table at my elbow, a small piece of inexpensive jewelry I hadn't missed.

"She give this. She say take back, huh? No can keep. I think Ana no thief. She hunt for you."

"I know."

The woman frowned. "How you know?"

I fished in my pocket. "This," I said and dropped the scrap of scarlet yarn beside the brooch. "I don't think she's a thief either. She came when I wasn't there and wanted something of mine. It's all right. I understand. Tell her I like her. But tell her next time not to tear up the rooms. There's no need. And she can have the pin. From me."

There was admiration in the big woman's eyes, and approval. "Lori good girl. One time Missy M. catch then— Poof! All finish. But I see Ana not bother 'gain, though. Not right." She shook her head positively. "No happen 'gain."

I might have a few other trinkets I could give the child. She had so little. Buried in the bottom of my small trunk was a string of beads— Memory struck me. The wallet! I'd forgotten all about it! I made my thanks and left, hurrying around the corner of the house and to the shrubbery. A puppy's growling stopped me. A spotted pup with floppy ears had the remnants of the wallet in his sharp little teeth and was tearing it unmercifully.

"Oh, no!" I cried. "What have you been up to?" I scooped the puppy into my arms, and he slapped at my chin with a warm red tongue. He wriggled to get down and I commenced gathering the shreds of leather—fortunately the part with the initials was intact—and wrapped the limp bits in my handkerchief. This time I would take it directly to Aunt Mellie; she'd know whose it was.

The little dog was busily snuffling at the ground, digging, his nose into the hole he had created and his forepaws sending out showers of earth between his hind feet. "Oh no," I said again, "now what are you after?" The end of a man's gold watch chain protruded from the hole, and I pulled it out gingerly. I brushed the soft dirt off the object, added it to the handkerchief, and rose with the pup in my arms.

Haines stood at the edge of the shrubbery, consternation showing on his face. He held out his hands; it was the pup he wanted.

"Mr. Haines?" I said. "I don't think he's been out very long. There must be a break somewhere, and puppies always dig."

He nodded and struggled with his words, then gestured, indicating he'd found the hole and patched it already. I pointed at the pup.

"May I carry him?"

What I was saying was understood well enough, for he stepped back a pace and preceded me down the path to the pens. Every one of the animals, and there were six, crowded to the fence, wagging their tails.

I handed over the pup and waited while Haines returned him to the pen, then knelt and held out my fingers to the nuzzling of friendly dog noses. These were the vicious brutes, I thought again.

I got to my feet and stood watching the puppy frisk about, his long ears flapping. I glanced up at Haines. "He's a bouncy little fellow. And cute! Is that his mother, the big brown one?"

Haines nodded; liveliness had come to the man's stolid features, and pitiful eagerness. How long had it been since anyone had taken the time or the trouble to treat him like a human being, to talk to him? "You take wonderful care of them," I said, "they look really good," and left him smiling as I walked away. The bundle in my handkerchief bumped gently against my thigh as I headed for the house.

"Where, exactly, did you get them?" Aunt Mellie demanded when I found her and showed her what I'd discovered. She poked at the damp leather with a bony fingertip. "And the chain—gold, too! My gracious, this is a shame. However could Mr. Swanson have gone off without them, I wonder? Though I am quite sure he must have had another chain, and if he needed the wallet too badly, he would assuredly have sent for it. Though as I say, it is too bad—I am afraid the wallet is quite spoiled. And you say some *dog* found them? What dog?"

I explained again patiently that the pup broke out, had been caught and returned to the pen.

"Make sure Haines secures it, then! He is responsible for the dogs, and it is his duty to see that they are confined at all times! I do not want any of those creatures running loose, is that clear?"

"I'm sure they won't," I hastened to reassure her. She had become very nervous. "There was only one small hole and the pup wriggled through. No one of the others made an attempt to get out, nor could have done if they wanted to. No, the pen is all secure and you have nothing to worry about."

Aunt Mellie nodded, she seemed satisfied, and except for her agitation over the dogs, seemed in a better frame of mind than I'd seen her for some time.

"The chain does belong to Mr. Swanson, then?"

"Oh yes. And the wallet also. The initials are right there, very plain, *S.S.* for Seivers Swanson. It must have lain in the earth a long time." Aunt Mellie sighed. "Mr. Swanson was very much the tropical plant fancier. He used to dabble about in the greenhouse section by the hour. He was working on some new type of fertilizer, he said, and appreciated our facilities. Possibly he laid the wallet down and forgot it. What was inside?"

"Nothing. No cards or anything. I saw the initials *S.S.*, then it fell apart in my hand."

"Sad." The old lady took off her spectacles, polished them mistily and then put them back on again, adjusting them on her nose. "Very sad. He was such an unhappy person, I often wondered what to do for him. *We* wondered. For that reason, though it was nice having company, we were glad to see him go. Thank you, my dear, for finding them."

"Will he be back this way again, do you think?"

"Oh no, I am certain not. He had a friend waiting for him, a Mr. Jackson—David Jackson, as I recall—and was on his way back to Africa—"

"I thought you said India. Wasn't that the D.J. you mentioned?"

"Who said?"

"Why, you did, at the table that night—"

"Oh dear, I guess I did. Why are you catechizing me like this? I am not on trial!" She'd turned suddenly still; there was something ominous about her smile, her eyes glittered dangerously.

With no stomach to become embroiled in another argument, I turned to leave the room.

"Where are you going?"

"I just thought—"

"Don't think! You're not supposed to think! You're a pretty sharp girl. What else have you found out around here?"

For a moment I was struck speechless, then I laughed lightly, trying to right a bad situation. "What should I know?"

"I think you are a prying creature, meddling in things that do not concern you! You wouldn't be here at all, except your father insisted."

My shoulders stiffened. "He what?"

"You heard me!" Aunt was not joking, none of this was a joke.

"So it wasn't your idea, but my father's? I might have known! Believe me, I wouldn't have foisted myself on you or on Montroth if I *had* known, never in the world have come if I hadn't thought you wanted me! A mistake not too late to rectify. I can leave right now if you like." My eyes stung with tears and I blinked them back furiously.

"Leave!" Aunt Mellie sneered. "How can you leave?"

I was surprised at the evenness of my voice. "I understand Jason drives down to Vancouver for supplies. Cook said he went last the eighteenth of February, almost three months ago. According to my calculations he should be going again tomorrow. I'm sure he'll take me. That should be satisfactory. I'll go pack my things."

"No, it is not satisfactory! And you will not pack your things! You flare up too fast—too fast! I told you to learn patience. Can't you take an old woman's idle words? I was only jesting!"

Jesting? I faced my aunt objectively. Why, this old lady was capable of anything! It was like looking at a stranger, someone I'd never seen before.

"You've made your position clear," I said and turned again. "I'd no idea any arrangement had been made. Don't worry, I won't ask you for a thing. I've sufficient means for my own support."

"You actually mean to go?" Aunt Mellie seemed stunned. "Leave us, when we've grown so fond of you? Why, you're all the life there is in this House! Always so cheerful, so happy. You can't go! There is no one else, we have no one, we would be entirely alone if you went. We—I—might as well be dead! Lorene, I know I am doing this badly—but can you understand what I am saying?"

An apology squeezing past the vinegar image? Aunt Lollie was frivolous, vain, but harmless; what about this one?

"You would be alone in the world without us, we would be alone without you. All we have is each other. Lorene? I have said many evil things in the past and regret them— can't we go on as before? And let there be no more talk of leaving!"

She was sincere; right now at any rate she meant what she said. It could not have been easy to come all the way down from ridicule to plea. I was still hurt and angry, but I went to her and put my arms around her bony little shoulders. "Very well, Aunt, if you really want me. And we will forget and start over again. All right?"

Perhaps she would not be so cutting after this. In taking my stand, maybe the tide had turned. Yet it would be hard to forget the one stunned moment in which I had so suddenly, completely, felt that I was in danger.

8

I COULD ACCEPT THE FACT that a wallet might be lost where a man was working, but a watch chain? How had it happened to be in the dirt? Could a chain chair, if detached from a watch, fall unnoticed from a waistcoat? Unlikely, but not impossible. I hadn't examined the chain to see if a link was broken. And how did it get buried? The ground was soft under the bushes, could summer and winter leaves and debris have drifted down over a period of time to cover it?

A minor mystery. A far more troubling one was the reason for the last confrontation with Aunt Mellie. No offense was meant, yet she'd flown into a violent rage. I still didn't know what I'd said to make her so angry. Had I reminded her of something better forgotten? It couldn't be that; D.J., at one time obviously a visitor to Montroth and the subject of dinner table conversation, was someone well known to both, and remembered by both with some fondness. It was beyond me. Either I'd missed something or wasn't getting the whole story. Yet standing up to her seemed not only to have cleared the air, but brought about peace as well. If only I could learn to take these eruptions in stride! To Aunt, they were a way of life, but they deeply disturbed me. While I struggled to put the episode aside, she had forgotten all about it.

With her suggestion that I shouldn't work so hard on the books in mind, I'd taken to going out more, following Jason around, helping him when I could. At first this distressed him greatly, but he soon grew to look forward to my visits.

I enjoyed myself so, that I often hurried to finish the tasks I had scheduled for myself in the library so I could go out. I spent a certain number of hours cataloguing, for despite Aunt Mellie's edict, I felt I owed the aunts that.

One afternoon I sat in the sunshine pulling weeds in the new flowerbed I'd suggested to Jason. Aunt Lollie was napping and Aunt Mellie didn't want to be disturbed.

I raised my face to the warmth and knew how a chrysalis must feel when it burst its bonds. Spring was truly here. Down in the pen the dogs argued desultorily; Haines raised his hand when he saw me then went on about his work. Jason was again back in the trees cutting firewood. This morning he had come to meet me, holding out a daffodil barely open.

Ana emerged from the back door, set a pan on the bench, smiled shyly, and withdrew. She hadn't taken off the yellow beads since I had given them to her.

I wished she could go somewhere where life was easier. Or at least that the aunts would share a bit of their largesse—a few decently fitted garments, a pair of pretty kid slippers to warm a girl's heart. But like royalty of old, they seemed to see little and care less for anyone or anything beyond their immediate surroundings and what concerned them personally.

The child probably missed Belinda, too. Belinda's departure had affected me strangely, my fear for her something I couldn't put into words. For days after she left I'd felt a deep sense of impending disaster. Her mother was ill, she'd said. But was that the real reason she'd gone? True, Montroth was remote, a long way out, but why had she turned evasive at my questions? It seemed to me the decision to leave had come about too suddenly. Had she seen or heard something? I didn't think so. Belinda was far too practical for that. I'd thought it might be the aunts, especially Aunt Mellie's tyrannical attitude, but she'd no direct contact with them; her orders came down from Narcisse, whom she understood very well. I could be making something out of nothing, I told myself; I should accept her simple explanation of sickness at home and let it go at that. But I knew I wouldn't rest until there was some word of her safety.

I looked up, studying the House. Crouched block-like and unappealing, it managed to convey the impression of dankness and gloom even in the bright light of day. On the second floor were my quarters, both aunts' on the third, the main balcony extending to serve both suites. My own balcony, by some error of construction, was considerably shorter, set off to one side, and could be reached only by a long step sidewise from my windows. Tacked on almost as an afterthought, I'd paid little attention to it before, nor considered its potential. But a chair, I thought, or a small ottoman if one were available, could be brought out, and I could create a jardiniere with ferns transplanted from the forest. It would marvelously lighten up the place, create a small soft island of greenness high in the air. Suddenly eager with planning, I jumped up and ran inside and to my room.

Holding my skirts carefully, I made the step to the balcony then stood to look. There wasn't much of a view, just trees. I remembered my first morning at Montroth, how eagerly I had scrambled from bed and pulled the heavy curtains aside to peer out, my eyes sweeping all those empty miles in disbelief.

Absorbed in my thoughts, I was conscious of no sound, no movement overhead until an object came hurtling down from above, directly at me. Instinctively I jerked aside, and a large flowerpot grazed my shoulder, then struck the railing, bounced off, and shattered on the driveway below. My heart in my mouth, I stared down, then up. There was no one on that balcony now, but the pot must have been pushed. Someone had done it—seen me standing and sent the heavy earthenware container down upon me.

Badly shaken, I retreated to my rooms to sink onto the bed and try to calm my jumping nerves. That railing had held two or three pots of varying sizes; the one that nearly hit me must have been the largest. But why—*why*? Someone trying to kill me? If the pot, falling from that height, had struck me directly, I could have been dead now or at least badly injured. There was no wind; this was one of the finest days we'd had. Even if the pot had been teetering on the edge of the broad railing, what were the chances of it falling at precisely the moment I was standing beneath it?

Forcing the weakness from my body, I stood up, walked back to the window, and looked out. I saw nothing of course, only the dreaming afternoon. Faintly, from far in the woods, I heard the crash of a tree as it went down; Jason would have felled it for more blocks of wood and knots to feed the hungry fireplaces. There was the slight rattle of china on a tray and a rustle of skirts as Hessit moved down the hall and to the stairs at the far end; it would be for Aunt Mellie, who demanded her hot peppermint tea daily at three on the dot. One could set his clock by that tea taking. Which, I knew, didn't rule out Aunt Mellie; she could have done it, couldn't she? and returned to her quarters in time. But why would she want to do me harm?

Allowing a few moments for Hessit to deliver the tray and again descend the stairs, I left my room and came silently to Aunt Mellie's door. I felt guilty creeping about so, but I steeled myself.

An ear against the panel verified the activity within. There was the unmistakable clink of pot against cup, cup against saucer, and a sharp exclamation at something not to her liking. Determined, I moved down the hall to Aunt Lollie's suite and repeated the performance.

Beyond this door, in her insufferably hot sitting room, Aunt Lollie was consulting her spirits. She had a "control," a Sir Basil, an eminent gentleman with whom she was now no doubt communing, for I heard entreaties, sighs, giggles.

I straightened impatiently—I couldn't see twittery little Aunt Lollie pushing down flowerpots! And Aunt Mellie might bluster, intimidate, challenge if she could, but do actual harm—no. I'd been wrong to suspect them. Each loved me in her own way and would never do anything in this world to hurt me. But who, then? It had happened. If I were to go to each of them and demand an explanation and nothing was gained by the questioning, what then? *Could* that pot have been precariously near the edge of the railing, and I just in the wrong place at the wrong time? I supposed stranger things had happened. Anyway, I decided to say nothing about it to anyone, but to watch. One thing I knew, I wouldn't go on that balcony again.

Grateful I still had my head on my shoulders, I descended the stairs, and since I had been gone from it for some considerable time—longer than I'd intended—sought the library and the work that always soothed me.

I handled the books carefully, sorting and putting aside those specimens whose covers and spines were bad. How my father would have loved to get his hands on them! A master at his craft, he would have painstakingly restored them to life, and loved every minute of it.

There was a gasp behind me. "Oh no! You are not supposed to—"

Startled, I turned. It was Aunt Lollie, a hand to her mouth and obviously horrified.

"Supposed to what?"

"Be in there—go in there." She pointed to the open door and the hallway beyond.

My back straightened with a snap and I forgot to be polite. "I don't know why not! There are books on those shelves, aren't there? And I'm here to catalogue. Nobody said I shouldn't—I didn't see any sign. And the door wasn't locked! I assumed it was part of my job."

"Oh yes, oh dear, of course." The curls bobbed. I could see now that she was attired in what was clearly her best, as if ready for a party. The scent of heliotrope lay heavy on the air. "I suppose you haven't done any harm. After all, what could you— No, I mustn't scold. You didn't know. But this is my sister's private store, and I'm sure she would not wish it disturbed in any way."

"All I want to do is clean things up, get these books sorted and put in some kind of order so they can be sold," I said gently.

"Sold!" The china-blue eyes flew wide. "But I don't know anything about that. I've never heard—are you sure? My sister told you?"

She had become very agitated, and I hastened to change the subject. Obviously she hadn't known; for some reason Aunt Mellie had not seen fit to tell her. "You came to see me? You wanted to see me about something?"

"Oh, yes, of course." She nodded vigorously. "For a moment I forgot! This quite put it out of my mind. You must come now, and we'll have our séance."

I hesitated, looking around the disordered room, the desk piled with my most recent armload of books. "I really would like to finish what I started. Maybe later—"

"Oh, please?" She clasped her bony little hands prettily against her chest, the cameo brooch quivering.

"All right," I agreed reluctantly. "You go ahead; I'll be along." I could have a few minutes for myself.

I waited until she was out of the room, then went through the hallway to the outdoors. The wind has risen, I noted as I found the bench and sat down. It would storm tonight. I let my wishes take me; memory tracing the strong lines of Stephen's face, the tallness that dwarfed me. He hadn't said when he would be back, but perhaps he didn't know. His work took him far and wide, he'd return the moment it was possible for him to do so. Wouldn't he? Why should I feel uncertainty now? He had asked many questions, evinced great interest in many things; the library, so much so I'd wondered at the time if books might be a particular diversion of his. Montroth was an antique, maybe he was taken with the place for its historical aspect. And the aunts—

certainly they were unique in their fashion, but— In spite of the warmth, the closeness I'd felt then, could I be sure it was I that had drawn him? He'd been on his way somewhere and stopped off at Montroth.

I deplored my traitorous thoughts, the doubts which were creeping in. Then a new uncertainty struck me with the force of a blow; Stephen said he saw me as he came up, Belinda that he'd asked where to find me. How could both be right?

The shrubbery rustled uneasily in the wind as if shaken by an unseen hand, and sharper gusts tugged at the tall bushes. The sky had darkened too. I looked up at the tops of those black swaying giants and a strange chill ran over me, some kind of warning I could not pinpoint or define. I struggled to throw off the dark fancies, telling myself it was just the impending storm that was causing my anxiety. Involuntarily I shuddered and looked behind me. Jason would come soon to close the hallway door and I should get back.

I rose to leave, then saw the small object in the grass almost at my feet—a length of printed paper crumpled as if tossed aside or fallen from a pocket. A railway schedule, I saw as I turned it over in my hand, bearing the date, January 1895. It had not been outside long, certainly not overnight or it would have been damp. That meant the schedule had been dropped recently, sometime today. I started at it with a sense of unreality. No one from this place would have need of such a thing! The aunts had not left Montroth, nor Haines, and Jason by wagon only. Could it be Jason's? He might have picked one up as he went through Moose Station. But for what reason? Foolishly, I thought of Stephen, wishing he had been so near.

The first splash of wet struck my hand; I put the schedule in my pocket and hurried inside, just as the rain began to fall in earnest.

Surely Aunt Lollie wouldn't mind waiting a few minutes longer; I lit the lamp so I could more closely examine my find. Of course there was no clue to its owner, there wouldn't be. Disappointed, I tucked it again into my pocket and bent to straighten an uneven stack of volumes on the desk; large books resting upon a smaller one.

I pulled out the small one—I'd not noticed it when I brought in the pile. It was leather-bound, bearing simply the word diary in gold stamp on its cover. Inside, there was an inscription in Aunt Mellie's spidery handwriting: *The Montroth Family. 1426 to—* The latter date was not indicated, from which I deduced that the diary continued up to the present time. Was this the record of family history that Aunt Mellie mentioned had been lost? I blew the dust off the book and adjusted the lamp, meaning to take only a quick look.

Amos Bedlington Montroth, began the first entry, *1426–1477. Cut down in the prime of life. Convicted assizes court, Murder.* Well, I thought, here was spice for the dull-as-ditchwater Montroth history, but I wondered if she would use it. My eye ran swiftly down the page. *Frances Culpepper Montroth, being a cousin to the above and no better administered to, 1430–1450. Arson. Later convicted Theft, Murder; beheaded, being but a public Specktacle. Lloyd Buddington Shreivers-Montroth, Sir; 1496–1524, Knighted 1523, executed 1524. Treason, Murder, Desertion.* I closed the book and placed it in the desk drawer, making sure the drawer was firmly closed. These people were long gone. Ancestors and their doings belonged to the dim past; I could even feel a breath of pity for unfortunate Sir Lloyd Buddington Shreivers-Montroth, knighted one year and executed the next. I blew out the lamp and ascended the stairs.

"You didn't expect me to be wearing a gown like this, did you?" Aunt Lollie greeted me as I entered. Again I was overwhelmed by the breathless heat, by the dim, lamplit room. Heliotrope and incense hovered nimbus-like around her. Lace fluttered at her neck and wrists, her bouffant pink skirts swept the floor, and the band of cerise velvet encircling her throat held a small exquisite pearl and garnet ornament.

"This dress was made for me many years ago and never worn. One must set the stage, you know. That is quite an outfit you have on; blue, isn't it?" She peered. "Nice, but so very plain. Don't you think you should have put on something a bit more in keeping?"

"Oh," I said, "I had no idea I was expected to." I glanced down at my dress, well-cut and well-fitted, with covered buttons and a neat tie at the neck. "I came directly here."

"Well—" Aunt hesitated. "I suppose it is all right. Perhaps you have nothing better anyway. What are you going to do with all the money? Mine and my sister's? I assume you will buy yourself some clothes. Pardon me for saying so, Lorene, but you do need them."

I hid a smile. Unless a garment bore frills, lace or feathers, it wasn't fit to wear. I said, gently stubborn, "To date I've made two wills for each of you, and none have been completed. But when you do make up your minds, leave me out of it. I'm not taking *anything*."

Aunt Lollie adjusted the lace at her cuffs, laughing lightly. "But my dear child, what will you do about it? And *I* am giving the most. Sister doesn't know that, but it's true. Dear Papa bequeathed me—but it is not important. Why, there is no one else to leave it to besides yourself. There will be this great handsome house and all of our possessions—of course you know their value even better than we do."

"Then I take it you own the property?"

Aunt looked pained. "But of course! Sister bought it outright many years ago. My dear girl, did you think that we— After all, the Montroths have never been—what is the term?—charity people. Now," she said, "we have talked quite long enough. Shall we get ready? You sit there in that chair, facing me. I am so glad you came!" The old lady giggled excitedly, her hands fluttering at her breast. "I feel very sure we will not be disappointed. Do you have anything in particular you wish to ask Planchette?"

Only how to get me out of this, I felt like saying, but aloud said hopefully, "Not that I can think of. Wouldn't you like me to read to you instead? I've a book you'd just adore." *Troilus and Criseyde*, I might have added, one of Chaucer's more flagrant excursions into the world of romance. "I could even tell you the story behind it. You see there was a girl named—"

"Gracious, not now. You see this is a special night. I am almost certain something wonderfully exciting is going to happen—"

"Cards, then?" Though I had the feeling my evasive tactics were getting me nowhere.

"But Lorene," Aunt appeared hurt, "I thought you looked forward to this as much as I! You must have some question, some request you wish to ask!"

"You really shouldn't depend on me," I murmured, "I'm much too down-to-earth for this sort of thing." I'd said it so many times. I eased resignedly into my chair while Aunt blew out the lamp and fussed over the candles, lighting them.

"See, how pretty?" She sat down opposite, instructing me in the procedure. Thus we remained, and nothing happened. The marker on the board was dead. Minutes passed. The wind rose, gusting against the house; rain, wind-driven, beat against the windows. The long vines—Aunt Mellie's and Aunt Lollie's vines, I didn't have any over my balcony— swished back and forth, back and forth with each change of the wind.

"Why do you have flowerpots on the balcony if you never use them?"

"Flowerpots on the—?" Aunt was clearly startled, and I could have sworn she didn't know what was behind my question. "Why, because they've always been there, I suppose."

"I don't smell mothballs in the house any more, but I did at first. Why?"

To this, she had an answer. "Oh, we used the last of those before you came. I guess we just never bought any more."

I had one further inquiry. "Would you know how often the railway schedules at Moose Station are issued? I mean, how many times a year?"

She stared at me. "What strange things you do ask! No, of course not. I don't know anything about—whatever you said. Now will you kindly pay attention to the business at hand? You've quite broken the chain!"

"I'm sorry," I mumbled, and again we sat motionless.

"Sir Basil is angry with us," the old lady murmured at last and flexed her bony fingers before placing them again on the heart-shaped indicator. "*I* am always so careful what I say and you should be, too. He is extremely sensitive. Lorene, do you hear music?"

"Only the wind."

"Footsteps?"

I smiled. How she was enjoying this! "A shutter banging somewhere."

"There are no shutters at Montroth Mansion!"

True; besides, it was a measured thump, a heavy thump. *And things that went clank in the night*? And it seemed to come from overhead. In spite of the smothering heat of the room, I shivered.

"Lorene, do you feel a draft? Surely you feel that!"

I did, all at once. The curtains behind the old lady swayed, and there was a distinct coolness about my ankles. One of the candles dimmed then grew bright again. Another candle flame flickered, suddenly wisping upward so only a pinpoint of blue remained. Smoke swirled upward in wreaths.

"This thing is not moving. Isn't it supposed to?"

"Lorene! You are just to keep your mind blank and let the spirits take us where they will. Lorene, what are you looking at?"

I couldn't have told her—my lips were stiff. Aunt jerked about like a marionette, following my gaze to face the window.

"What is it—oh, what is it? What are you looking at—I can't see, the light is too bad!" She was now staring fearfully at the widely-billowing lavender drapes and the yawning blackness beyond. The windows were open! One of the candles guttered and died.

"The candle—the other one—shut the window!" Aunt shrilled. She stumbled to her feet and stood trembling, her hands clasped tightly before her.

There was a scrape, a thud from the balcony outside, and an object skittered across the roof. Aunt Lollie uttered a choked gasp and fell in a faint at my feet.

Reaching for the windows I halted; the one remaining candle flame flared upward, swirled, and went out. Even as I stood in the stygian darkness, the scrape and thump came again. I clawed my way to the windows and by touch only, slammed them closed—I had to have light. I didn't know where the matches were, and I needed light. Stumbling over Aunt's inert body, I plunged for the door, my fingers encountering the bellpull. The bell jangled throughout the house. I stood, my shoulders pushed hard against the wall, until Hessit came running. "Not me," I gasped, "Aunt Lollie—go *on*!"

It was a million miles down the hallway and down the stairs. I imagined something cold and clammy slapping at my back, clutching at my heels. I burst into my room as if all the furies were after me. Then stopped short. My own windows were open! Hadn't I closed and locked them securely? The force of the storm could have— But what explanation was there for the wet impress on the carpet—in front of the chair pulled up to the fire, where wet feet might have rested against the fenders? Tracks? Big ones. All at once the room didn't feel like a shelter any more. I whirled and ran out the door, and stood until my heart slowed its beat and I could draw free breath again.

Reentering that room was the hardest thing I ever did. I'd left a lamp burning on a corner table; air swooping in had blackened the wick and sent the flame climbing up the chimney. The windows were rattling furiously, the curtains flung wide; rain, wind-driven, made a wet path in direct line to the fireplace and the blotches before the fenders. There were no tracks!

9

THE LAST BRUSH with the supernatural almost pushed Aunt Lollie over the brink. She was hysterical and weeping by turns. The séance had done nothing for my peace of mind either, but for Aunt to be so certain that the disembodied consciousness of some former visitor to Montroth had returned and meant in some demonic fashion to do her ill—this seemed foolish in the extreme. Without a doubt it was one of the strangest and most stupid fixations I'd ever heard. It was true the old lady's mind prowled far afield—and not without some cause, I was beginning to believe—but this was most incredible. By daylight, I'd carefully examined the balcony outside my window, finding several shingles torn loose by the wind. And on the ground, I'd discovered branches of varying sizes, one quite large. Shingles, ripped from their mooring, could skitter across a roof, branches stripped from trees and flung against the house by the force of the gale, could create thumps and scrapes.

The vines, certainly sturdy enough, covered almost the entire front of the house, but there was no man on the place sufficiently agile to climb them to the third floor, or even the second. And since when had ghosts taken to climbing vines and leaving wet footprints on carpets? I tried to explain to Aunt Lollie, but she wouldn't listen. Maybe I wasn't convincing enough; maybe I only half believed my logical explanations myself. It would be a long time before

I could forget the near-panic that drove me from that room. Perfect tracks!

Aunt Mellie, too, took alarm. She had Jason up to double-check the locks on the doors, and upon her express order, the windows were to be kept shut and bolted at all times. Still shaken myself, I nevertheless felt this was going to extremes. Lovely, mild, late spring weather was upon us and even finer weather was to come; two aged hothouse plants wouldn't miss soft breezes and balmy air, but I had no intention of abiding by such a command.

Hessit faithfully attended Aunt Lollie, but the Jamaican woman no longer took Aunt Mellie's orders without question. She had acquired a grim determination that was most evident. Something had sent her from Aunt Mellie's room with an aroused awareness that prompted her to watch over me at all times. I couldn't understand it. With some self-reliance of my own, such hovering tried my patience. When Hessit insisted upon carrying my meals to me, I rebelled.

The entire household seemed to have fallen under some strange spell. Aunt Lollie was rarely seen outside her suite, and when the dogs howled, she cowered in her bed, calling pitiably for me. Frivolous as she was, I felt deeply sorry for her. Her terror was genuine, and she was half-demented by fear. I actually worried that in one of her weeping attacks she might go mad completely. The Presence had returned once and could again, she repeated over and over, frequently going on about her "sins." Upon these occasions, protest as I would, I was gently but firmly ushered from the room by Hessit.

A change marked Aunt Mellie too. She no longer demanded my presence at table, in fact most of the time she failed to put in an appearance herself. Moreover, she was even more unpredictable, and I never knew, day or night, when I might be called upon for some trivial chore—to fetch a book, a scarf or handkerchief, to rouse Cook to make a pot of tea. For some reason, Aunt Mellie was more deathly afraid of the dogs than before, and I was often summoned wearily from my bed to sit with her. It came to me that stubborn little Aunt Mellie, whether she admitted it or not, was in her way seeking human warmth against some terror of her own.

I was expected to spend two hours of each day, and more if I could manage it, with Aunt Lollie. Occasionally I brought some tidbit from the kitchens, and sometimes fed her with my own hands. But when it came to the Cozy Corner I was adamant. Her coaxing fell on deaf ears.

"No," I would say firmly. "I'll play cards with you, play dominoes with you, play tiddlywinks with you, but no more séances." I couldn't understand why she'd want to have one, but it was her affinity for Sir Basil, of course.

Aunt Mellie was not backward about making it clear that she bitterly resented these visits to her sister, and I was finding it increasingly difficult to get back on equable footing with her.

On the twenty-sixth of May there was a sudden unexpected flurry of snow and to my surprise Aunt Mellie— not Aunt Lollie—took to her bed with the sneezes and violent cramps. Upon hearing that her sister was down, Aunt Lollie bounced back admirably; she took up knitting and crocheting again, and was to be found any hour of the day cheerfully before the fire, little feet tucked up on her footstool, knitting and smiling like a cat over a saucer of cream. Fortunately for me, she napped a lot, too.

When I could, I escaped to the kitchens. On this particular morning I was met with the demand that I learn to cook.

"Look—Narcisse show. Make biscuit. Good! Learn, huh?"

Rapidly and expertly she assembled ingredients and utensils, even as I edged toward the door. "See, then do," the huge woman commanded. She stood with arms akimbo and scowled at my reluctance. "Got learn to cook," she scolded. "Man all time hungry, all time eat. Full belly, much happy. Cook 'tato, soup, cook meat. Today biscuit, so get busy."

I supposed the reference to a man's appetite, in Narcisse's heavy-footed way, hopefully placed a marriage somewhere in my future. The concern was well-meant, and I could only go along with her demands.

"What do I do?" I asked helplessly. I'd never been faced with flour and lard and been expected to turn them into biscuits.

"Put here—in here." Narcisse pointed. "All measure, jus' put. Mix, like so." She illustrated. "A'right?"

Ana came in and paused, rooted to the floor in surprise at my activities. I explained and wasn't sure whether she understood or not, but she nodded. Narcisse extended a pan, Ana was·to fetch apples from the root cellar. "For pie." Narcisse waved a hand. "An' applesauce. Jason, Haines, he eat in kitchen, him like applesauce. Go now," she said to the girl, who still stood.

It wasn't easy and I didn't get much help, but at last I sat down with fresh coffee, to wait while my biscuits baked.

"Snow all gone," Narcisse said by way of conversation. "Fast come, quick go."

I smiled. "A French-Canadian saying?"

"Narcisse say. Too late in year. Make sense? Little bit, maybe yes. Melt, good for garden."

I fingered my coffee cup. Narcisse refilled it and poured one for herself, then sat down opposite me. "You like dem two old lady?" she asked abruptly.

"Why," I replied, astonished at the question, "yes. Of course. Well—they're not always easy to understand, but—Why?"

"Not'ing. Not'ing." The Indian woman shrugged. "Narcisse jus' wonder. Forget I say, huh? Lori good girl, Lori not get hurt." She repeated grimly, "Narcisse see Lori not get hurt."

"But," I demanded, "why should I get hurt? This is a crazy place, maybe, but nobody ever set out to hurt me—" I hesitated, remembering the heavy pot hurtling down at me. "Narcisse," I said, "I think the dogs' howling bothers you too. You've been listening to them too much and letting it get to you. And while we're on the subject, there is something I want to ask. Why aren't the dogs ever let out to run?"

"No. Dog dig—here, there. Dig. Got garbage pit out back."

"I *know* that," I retorted. "But why couldn't Jason or Haines fence off the garbage pit—"

"*Non*," Narcisse stated flatly. She got up, turned her back and began lumbering about her chores. "Narcisse got work now," she grunted. "No sit talk all day. No ask more questions, huh? Lori go now. Come back later get biscuit."

I shook my head. Let the men have them; biscuits would be good with applesauce. The main thing was that I had made them.

The atmosphere could change quickly in this part of the house too. I stepped to the back porch, more and more puzzled. I'd struck a nerve somewhere. The dogs? I hardly thought so. For some reason Narcisse was touchy about the garbage pit; I couldn't think why. It was logical that the animals were not let out; naturally they would dig, and I could imagine the resulting mess. But I still thought fencing off the pit was a good idea.

The big cellar door had been boarded up tight, ordered so by Aunt Mellie immediately after I'd searched for, and found, my necklace. With the insect spray stored elsewhere, she'd stated crisply, there was no need for further entry. She need have no concern about me. I wouldn't have gone into that cellar again if my life depended upon it. Even now, just looking at the door my skin crawled and a chill swept over me. The place had a feeling all its own, like a breath from a grave. Coupled with the rats, the heap of refuse—

What *was* all that spray used for? Every tree in the orchard was so mossy and infected with scab I'd thought they were dead. Surely no treatment had touched them for years. And the dog pens—they were always kept scrupulously clean. Haines cut wild hay to spread on the floor of the shacks used as kennels and daily brought in armloads of aromatic balsam boughs for the yard. I knew without asking that no disinfectant was used. The only possible explanation for the great amount of the material was the vast distance between Montroth and civilization. All supplies were bought in quantity.

The morning air was fresh and clean. The thin snow of the night before had completely vanished—there was not a whisper of it left. The earth breathed warm under the sun as though no snow had fallen at all. The azaleas were out, the rhododendron buds bursting red.

Ana came over with the pan of apples, chose the largest, scrubbed it vigorously on the front of her dress and held it out to me. On the point of refusing, I smiled and accepted the fruit. She turned at the door and lifted a hand and I waved back. I was glad for this contact, and greatly pleased at the protectiveness Narcisse showed toward the girl.

I went around the house and entered by the side door. It was very quiet; both aunts must be sleeping late, I thought. It was a reprieve, and I gravitated to the library. I hadn't been able to do much work here lately—like a seesaw, when one aunt was down the other was up—and everything was exactly as I had left it.

Aunt Mellie and Aunt Lollie had been well aware of George's visit. Aunt Mellie, outraged, had appeared briefly at the stair landing to glare down at us, and she would have told her sister of the stranger's intrusion. The two so strongly resisted contact with Outside, but what about those visitors to Montroth over the years? They came, were graciously received, and went their way.

"Lorene." I looked up; Aunt Mellie, still a bit weak but vastly improved, stood in the doorway. "Where have you been? Breakfast is in the dining room."

"Will you be joining me?" I said in surprise.

"Hessit is bringing a tray. I'll be down later." She must have just risen, there were still curlpapers in her hair.

I nodded and went on to the dining room. A huge tureen on the sideboard held hot corn muffins and there was honey in a small cut glass dish. Another tureen contained breaded cutlets, and nearby, a variety of condiments. There was the steaming pot of tea. I filled a plate and ate in solitary splendor, seated alone at the end of the long table.

The meal finished, I returned to the library. Alone, I let my mind wander, my thoughts centering on what was deepest in my heart—Stephen. I was in love with him. Did he have feelings for me? What he said made me think so. He couldn't forget, he'd said. He would have come no matter how far. Were they only pretty words, spoken, then forgotten? When he kissed my hand, lightly and beautifully, was it a gentleman's politeness, not to be taken too seriously? Or a gesture meant to carry a warm reminder that there was something more to be treasured between us?

I'd dreamed about Stephen last night. I was walking a very narrow plank across a terrible morass. It was nearly dark and the mud under the plank was black ooze. Stephen stood on the far bank, waiting. I tried to see in the gloom, but slipped. Falling, I cried out for help, but he backed away, and faded. I had never been troubled by dreams or worried if they had meaning, but this was so clear, so real! In spite of this, and my doubts, I made a determined effort to lay it all aside.

I returned to my work—Cicero, Mallory, Shakespeare. Some time passed, then I heard a sound behind me and turned. Aunt Lollie stood pale and swaying in a lavender wrapper and maribou mules, the odor of heliotrope strong in the air.

"Aren't you well? Here, let me help—" I sprang to empty a chair of its assorted volumes, but I was waved aside.

"I'm—fine. My dear, don't worry about me. I always recover. But in case one of these times I do not, I want your help. My sister has been monopolizing you, hasn't she? And she will, so long as you allow it. She's a despicable autocrat, incredibly selfish, thinking only of herself. She

knows I want some time with you, but will she allow me
equal opportunity? Not she! And I will tell you something,
Lorene—my sister is *crazy*. Yes, that is true. She only has
spells of lucidity. I've long suspected it, but now I know.
She has always had such tendencies, but has been getting
worse of late years. And in her jealous madness she means
to keep you at her side every moment, no matter what anyone else's wants or feelings might be. Watch out for her! I
am giving this as a warning. She could be dangerous."

No, I thought, this was too much. The pot calling the
kettle black. Each sister accusing the other of madness. I
tried to break in, but Aunt went babbling on.

"I need some of your time and find I must take it. I, too,
have my rights! Please come to my room. I want to make
a will."

I gaped. "Another one? But you've already made—"

"Now." She was in no condition to argue, and I hardly
in a position to refuse. I followed her, but not willingly.

Once more as the door to her room opened there was the
blast of trapped heat. The dead air hovered so thick and so
heavy it clogged the lungs, the cloying scent of heliotrope
overpowering. I longed to throw the windows open and
breathe deeply of the freshness outside.

"Thank you, my dear, for coming. Now I expect you
would like to get right down to business." Aunt floated
across the room and picked up a paper from her desk. "I
confess I am feeling better, perhaps it is your visit that has
done it."

I took down what I was told to and a half hour later
we were finished. From what I knew of wills, this one,
like the others, was correct in every respect, but like the
others, no beneficiary's name had been filled in. An omission which then, as now, appeared to bother her not at
all.

Aunt Lollie's china-blue eyes gazed at me hopefully, the
little hands clasped to the flat breasts in a familiar gesture.
"I was so disappointed that Sir Basil did not visit us the

other night. But of course, the storm—" She shuddered delicately. "There are many of them, my friends of course, but Sir Basil is the main one. He is such a—so *faithful*. He always comes when I call, always, and before any of the others. I am sure it is because he has such fine regard for me. Sir Basil was a member of the House of Lords in life, you know, very highly placed and of excellent character. Truly a man due great respect."

I knew what she wanted and remained unmoved. "Ah, well," she sighed, "and we hardly gave him a chance. A very grave pity! But I have something you must see. Just a moment while I get them—" She pulled albums bulging with photographs from a small cabinet, and I sighed inwardly. But what could I say? They meant so much to her.

The photos were of family groups, the people strangers to me, austere souls. The stiff poses were all the same: the men seated in front, women with babies in their arms beside them, children ranged by age at their parents' knees. Almost invariably the boys were in knee-length velvet suits with stiff lace collars, the little girls copies of their mothers in voluminous dresses, heavily beribboned and buttoned, with just the toes of their small shoes peeping out. In the photos of the newly-married, the husband was always grim, sturdily seated, the wives standing straight, dedicated, and obedient, behind him with a hand on his shoulder. I half-listened to Aunt Lollie prattle on. This was Aunt Hester, this Uncle James, Benjamin and Aretha at the front. Here were Aunts Penelope and Mary Margaret with Uncle Charles David. He was knighted, you know.

"Before our trouble," Aunt Lollie said wistfully, "we spent our summers with Mama and Papa at Uncle's estate in Surrey. My! it was lovely. Then poor Mama died, and Papa—" She shrugged her little shoulders. "I don't suppose you want to hear about that anyway. It was *very* bad trouble, you understand. And they actually found out that all the time Papa had been—but he was clumsy, I will say that for him. No finesse! Now you take my sister—" Aunt broke off abruptly, shaking her head. "No, I mustn't discuss that. So tiresome, at any rate."

I didn't have the slightest idea what she was talking about.

Aunt Lollie laid one album aside and reached for another. She eyed me sternly. "Your friend didn't stay long, did he?" I was surprised. She meant George, of course.

"My sister was most dreadfully upset. As I was, also! Lorene, you simply do not understand that we cannot have company—we do not *want* company. You were not a good girl to bring him here."

I opened my mouth to protest but closed it again. What was the use? I could have asked about the visitors they'd had themselves, but didn't do that either.

When Hessit knocked and entered with tea, I was vastly relieved. "I'm sorry," I murmured, and made my retreat.

The dogs howled that night. One began it, then every other throat burst into a violent explosion of sound. It was a frenzied, unanimous uproar as they fought to free themselves of their prison and get at—what? What was out there? Secure behind my own locked door, I still felt the night pressing in. How must the others of Montroth be faring? The old ladies who surely needed their rest? I'd voiced that concern before, to Belinda, and now it occurred to me again. Perhaps the pens should be moved far back in the forest. But that wouldn't do; no outcry like this one could be far enough away not to be disturbing.

The racket continued for a long time, but at last began slowly to abate, one animal after the other subsiding into barks and finally into snarls. Then there was silence, so utter and complete the walls seemed to throb with it.

Sleep was out of the question; hot milk might help. It wasn't long past midnight because the room was warm; the fire in the fireplace had barely bitten into its night load of knots.

I hesitated after opening my door and paused on the threshold. The long hall was dark. I moved carefully, feeling my way toward the stairs, then halted, listening. A footfall? A loose board? I scoffed at my anxiety. It was only the sound of an old house settling.

My fingers reached for the railing, but I could not find it. I moved a pace forward, then something behind me seemed to touch, to push; my foot caught and I catapulted down the stairs.

Arms outflung, rolling over and over, I clutched wildly at the balusters—anything to save myself, to break my fall— and came up short, halfway to the bottom.

I was first felt wonder that I'd survived the plunge, that I had managed to stop myself and not gone all the way to the floor below. Disoriented, I lay where I was for long moments until my head stopped spinning and my heart began to resume its normal rhythm. My own quarters seemed the safest haven, and I rose at last, still badly shaken. Holding hard to the railing, I slowly made my way back up the stairs and to my room.

Had someone been waiting at the top of the steps? Had someone pushed me? Or had I caught my heel somehow in the carpet and that caused me to tumble?

ᑫᔆ 10 ᑫᔆ

THERE WAS A HOLE in the carpet at the head of the stairs. Examination revealed a frayed spot resulting from wear, but torn larger when my heel caught. The rough edges were smoothed down, a few tacks added, and that was that.

Some of the floor coverings at Montroth were old, and over the years had required patching, but no one had any notion at all that the carpet was so worn in this particular place. It could have been disastrous. I was lucky to escape serious injury! What was I doing walking about in the dark, anyway, they asked. I explained, and explained again.

How could it have been anything other than what it appeared to be—an accident? Who could I blame? I had actually seen no one. The slight push on the back, just enough to tip me off balance and send me hurtling down the steps, was all imagined.

But I couldn't help wondering. I'd gone up and down those stairs upon countless occasions and seen no worn area; Hessit traversed the halls constantly; Aunt Lollie and Aunt Mellie both crossed the landing to reach their third-floor quarters.

There must be something to the warnings—first Hessit's, then Narcisse's. The flowerpot—suppose that wasn't an accident? A push at the head of the stairs—suppose the carpet had been cut? I hadn't thought so, but it could have been. Strange that such a ragged hole would suddenly appear, when there was none before. Why should these things be happening to me? I had no enemies, as far as I knew.

I could creep about, testing every corner, every shadow for danger, or hold my suspicions in check, get on with my life, and be on my guard.

Then something happened to put even this out of my mind. I'd started the day as usual, worked for a while, then with neither of the aunts having put in an appearance, breakfasted in the kitchen with Narcisse. Ana was on the porch peeling potatoes, and she smiled back over her shoulder at me. I had given her several small trinkets, a chain to wear with the beads, ribbons for her hair, a bracelet of inexpensive gold wash, with a round gold stone set in the top. This, and the yellow beads, she always wore.

"You want learn to cook some more?" Narcisse asked. "Make pudding."

I shook my head. "Not this time." I pushed back my plate. Breakfast could be very pleasant here, warm, with the smells of food cooking. Often Jason or Haines came in, and occasionally Hessit appeared; there was life and activity.

"Lori worried. What worried 'bout?"

"No, it's nothing." The big woman looked at me keenly, and I had the feeling she was seeing beneath the surface. I told her I'd found a railroad schedule, and asked if she knew who had lost it.

Narcisse shrugged, it was clear she was at a loss. She said maybe it had been Belinda. But Belinda had left sometime before the schedule was lost. It had to be Jason's then.

"Did you hear the dogs last night?"

Narcisse frowned. "Who not hear dogs? Dam' dogs, bark too much, no sleep."

"What were they barking at?"

The question caught her by surprise. Was there sudden caution in her manner—the same diffidence that Belinda had shown?

"I no know. Their own selves, maybe, or deer—"

"There aren't that many deer in the woods," I stated flatly. "Narcisse, if you know something, why don't you tell me? What is it? They wouldn't bark like that at Haines, and they surely wouldn't at Jason. And they don't bark that way at me. They don't make any such uproar when Ana goes out to bury the garbage. The only time I ever heard them make that kind of a racket at *anybody,* was when Belinda dragged the knots, and they didn't know who it was. They're so nervous, on edge all the time, but only at night. When I go out there during the day, they can't wait to get to me, wagging their tails. Are you sure you don't know what's setting them off?"

Narcisse rested her big hands on the table and leaned forward, facing me. "Lori not know all them things in woods. Is skunk. Is raccoon. Is bear—yes, bear. Bear curious, like to snoop. Is *carcajou*—him wolverine. Bad actor. Dog hate, *carcajou* hate dog, tear to pieces if can get at. Dog, him go crazy when smell wolverine. And is wolf. I think wolf. Many small things. No take much for dogs to bark. Lori understan'?"

Somehow the explanation failed to satisfy. How often did these "small things" venture out of their native habitat to roam unfamiliar, man-smelling places? Not as often as these dogs howled, I was sure. But it was all the answer I was going to get. Narcisse refused to discuss the subject further.

"I think I'll take a walk," I said, and unfolded from my stool. I could feel Narcisse watching me narrowly. She had put me off and I knew it. Why? She must have some reason for the evasion.

"Lori?"

I turned at the door. "Yes?"

"Is all right. Everything going to be fine, so no worry no more, huh? You listen now, Narcisse say. All be fine. No worry 'bout *nothing*."

I nodded. Unlike Belinda, Narcisse doled out her favor very sparingly. It was something to appreciate. I didn't want to go back into the main house, not yet anyway. The books could wait. There had been no further mention of a sale, and when I'd suggested that as a preliminary we should have someone in to evaluate the collection, the proposal was coolly ignored. Maybe they had changed their minds and decided to keep the books; in any event, it was not my place to push the matter. At least the library would be in better order than it was when I came.

I didn't see Jason, so I moved past the shrubbery and presently into the path to the conservatory. The windows were as unwashed and as cobwebby as before; the same unkempt vines clawed fingers against the glass, their dry stems now crowded by this year's lush new growth.

How long was it since anyone had used this place? Montroth had gone to seed, I thought, and everything connected with it. If only the dark cloud which seemed to hover over Montroth could be lifted! I had an odd sense of finality, even about Aunt Mellie and Aunt Lollie. Something was coming to an end, good or bad I could not have told. Perhaps, I thought with distant hope, Stephen Landrau would come back and set all things to rights. Maybe it was company I needed, maybe it was company we all needed.

Mr. Swanson had worked in this greenhouse, when it was a greenhouse. Hadn't Aunt Mellie said he was involved in perfecting a plant fertilizer? I walked the single long aisle up, and returned; trays, benches, broken pots, and a few spears of what might once have been plants, were all that remained. Here was where I found the wallet, but there was no further evidence that Mr. Swanson had been, or ever worked, in this place. No utensils, no cans, no buckets—nothing.

I turned to leave, and was suddenly depressed by an odor, vague but remembered, and raised my eyes to stare at the jugs and jars ranging along the high shelf above me. The deep scent of mold was with me once again; in the gloom the rustle of small furry creatures was chittering around my feet; in the air was a breath out of a sepulcher, filled with horror and with death—

I gasped and turned blindly for the door, and ran outside. What had come over me? I'd been like one possessed. It was only an abandoned building, I told myself, what had it to do with horror and death? Aunt Lollie would have cowered and said it was inhabited by some restless spirit, but I should be saner.

The House was waiting, and this time I did not shrink to see it. I hurried to the nearest door and let myself inside.

Aunt Mellie was in the drawing room, and she swung to me at once. "Where were you?"

I'd collected myself and was able to speak in a normal tone. "I was out in the conservatory."

"What were you snooping around there for?"

"I don't know why you call it snooping," I replied with some asperity. "First you told me to get acquainted with the place, investigate its corners, even the secret passages, now you seem annoyed that I went back to the conservatory. I found only one secret passage—"

"There is only one! And you would do well to stay out of that. Breakfast is in the dining room."

"I've already eaten," I said, "but I'll have tea with you—"

"Already eaten? The kitchens again, I'll be bound. You should not fraternize with the servants, Lorene! I assumed you were taught better."

My shoulders stiffened. "I like Narcisse," I said firmly. "And I like Jason and Haines and Hessit. And Ana. They are all *people*. Which reminds me of something I've been wanting to ask—Ana needs shoes. And I think that rag of a dress she is wearing is the only one she has. Couldn't we—"

Aunt's eyes had widened, then narrowed. "No, we can't! It's enough that she has food in her belly. I did not ask for her in the first place, did not want her."

Like me? I almost said. I clenched my teeth. You're not exactly a likable creature, I thought. If you weren't my aunt I'd— Whatever the threat, it was left unfinished. I managed to say calmly, "I could stand a cup of tea."

"Have your tea, then, though it is probably cold by now. If so, ring for Hessit. It is Cook's duty to see food properly presented. Hessit is bringing a tray to my rooms. I'll be down later."

Without another word, she left. Another pointless demand—don't go in the conservatory. I had already been in the hallway, investigated its books, found the diary. Obviously she'd found it too; the last time I looked the diary was gone from the drawer where I'd put it.

My temper strained to the breaking point, I took stock of myself. Where was the comradeship I'd felt upon coming to this House? The pity? The patience I'd been determined to show? I should understand that these two were *old*, that they could be forgetful, or remembering, be hateful, even vindictive. That the animosity they showed each other was the result of years and circumstance.

I had my tea, and catalogued some books. When Hessit went by on her way upstairs, I caught her and asked if she could cut down one of my dresses, even two, for Ana. The Jamaican woman nodded, eager to comply. I only hoped it wouldn't place too great a burden on Hessit. Had I been in her position, I would already be footsore from running between two old ladies.

I wasn't too surprised at Aunt Mellie's dismissal of responsibility for Ana, still the curt declaration stung me. It would have taken so little!

With an idea in mind, I went to Aunt Lollie's quarters. After disabusing her of the notion that I'd relented and come for a séance, I got on with what I had to say.

"But gowns, my dear—you cannot mean that!" She was quite horrified, I saw. "Why, I don't have a single one that—I'm sure you understand. I simply wouldn't hear of parting with any of them. Some girl somewhere, you say? What girl? I know of no girl. In need, in this House? You must be mistaken. At any rate you do appreciate my position, don't you? Now if you wanted something for yourself I might loan, but I wouldn't dream of—"

I understood. Of course I did. She stood before me in fine Brussels lace and cerise velvet. I nodded politely and got out.

I didn't have much to choose from. Aunt Lollie was right about the state of my wardrobe. There was ample for myself, but finding something suitable to alter for a young girl was difficult. I rummaged through and finally managed to come up with a dark blue bombazine, quite full; a morning skirt, also full; and two waists with nice collars and buttons. A far cry from what I had in mind, but anything Hessit could turn out would be a vast improvement over what Ana now had. I would have clothed her in pink. I knew pink was not *apropos*, but could imagine how a child's heart would yearn for something bright and pretty.

I returned to my work in the library. A short while before noon Aunt Mellie came downstairs. She looked rested and almost festive, with a crisp white frill at her throat and her thin hair freshly done. I was about to remark that she seemed in fine high spirits, when Hessit, agitated, appeared suddenly in the doorway. Jason, gently supporting a figure in his big arms, pushed past her.

"*Stephen!*" I cried. "What's the matter—oh, what's the matter?"

It was probably the first time for as long as she'd been at Montroth that Narcisse had entered the dining room. "Him horse, he step in hole, fall. Bad fall. Hurt ribs. Bust! Jason find and bring in. He—man, better be fixed up. You fix, Missy, huh?"

Stephen had straightened painfully, holding himself in. His eyes sought mine. "Sorry. Had a little trouble back down the trail."

"Missy?" Narcisse persisted urgently.

But Aunt Mellie stood stiff and resistant, her face hard and ungiving. "Who is this man? Never mind, take him away! I won't have him in my house! Take him out, I say!"

The certainty that had been in Jason's eyes faded, the warmth retreating, and I had the feeling he was seeing Aunt Mellie for the first time. Without another word he turned, and again supporting Stephen, left the room. Far away I heard the back door slam.

I faced her, incredulous. Gone were my good resolutions, the patience I'd determined to show. "Aunt Mellie, how could you!"

"You know that man? Who is he?"

I heard my words, cold and very, very deliberate. "His name is Stephen Landrau. And yes, I know him. He came to see me—"

"Here?"

"Yes, here!"

"Why wasn't I told?"

"Why should I tell you? I was afraid to! Wouldn't you have acted the way you're doing now?"

She ignored the question.

"And that other—person. You had him here. Uninvited, or so you said! I told you Letitia and I will not tolerate strangers poking about the house!"

"But this is different!" I still didn't quite believe she was so heartless. "He's hurt! And you refuse him shelter? I don't understand this at all! How—could—you!"

I could have continued, but it wouldn't have done any good. As far as she was concerned, Stephen didn't exist. Her eyes glittered, and I thought for a moment she was going to strike me. Then her hand fell stiffly to her side and she stalked from the room. She would never give in, never bend. The gentleness I'd seen was an illusion, a notion, a mood. She would never be anything but a hard, choleric old woman, devoid of the milk of human kindness.

I sought Narcisse. She was tearing a sheet into strips. "For wrap chest," she said. "Jason, he fix. Lori no worry, be fine."

"But how is he?" My words tumbled over one another. "I mean—"

Narcisse called over her shoulder to Ana, the girl shrinking back into the shadows of a corner. "Fill teakettle for fresh coffee, an' hurry up!" To me she said with a gentleness in her voice I'd not heard before, "Not good. Have to stay flat on back one week, maybe two. That way, ribs no puncture lung. But Jason good, he know how to fix up chest, wrap nice an' snug. Jason take care of, you no worry."

"But I saw—"

The big woman shook her head sharply. "Narcisse know what you saw. Now you no never mind, huh? Something go on here Lori got no part of. Lori stay out of the way, think good thoughts. By-an'-by maybe go see sick one. But not now! Lori go on 'bout her business."

I took a deep breath, I was still shaking inside. But what she said made sense. I tried to recall all I'd heard about broken ribs. Stephen's horse had thrown him. Was Stephen on his way to see me when it happened? My thoughts churned.

"But where will he stay? Aunt Mellie refused to take him in—"

Narcisse had a big pile of strips. Jason came to the back door, nodded satisfaction, and turned with the pile in his arms to smile reassurance at me. Tears stung my eyes at the gesture. Whatever Jason knew of nursing, he would do the very best he could.

"See?" Narcisse said as Jason disappeared. "He fix fine. Just take time, now. Give ribs chance to heal. Lay quiet, no be disturb' 'bout anything. Eat. Sleep. Rest. Narcisse cook, feed him up good. He young an' strong, bones heal nice, but must stay in bed. Have Jason's room in lean-to. Jason fix up 'nother for self in shack off barn."

"I would like to go see—"

"*Non*! Maybe later, all right? Leave be now! Let rest. Lori go, Narcisse got work to do."

Once again I was dismissed. I glanced toward the barn and lean-to. Stephen was out there and I— But however strongly I might feel, no matter how badly I wanted to be with him, Narcisse was right. He needed to rest, to lie still and relax as much as he could. And with Stephen so near, there would be tomorrow and tomorrow—

～ 11 ～

I DIDN'T SEE STEPHEN for three days. Not because I didn't want to, for every moment of every hour I yearned to be at his side, but because I was firmly instructed to wait. His body was very sore, he was in pain, he must not move even the slightest bit. I was told to let him settle down after the accident, then I could go. Jason was taking good care of him.

In the meantime, the atmosphere in the mansion was cool. My conversations consisting of "Yes, Aunt Mellie," or "No, Aunt Mellie." Upon one occasion, Aunt Lollie came down to dinner in ruffles and lace, and trailing scent. If she knew of the arrival of the stranger, she gave no hint. She said little, seemed preoccupied, and left at once when the meal was finished.

"Twiddling with her spirits again. She'll go down, mark my words. Serve her right for dabbling with the devil, addleheaded old fool." Aunt Mellie's derisive shot was hurled at Aunt Lollie's retreating back. The benign smile Aunt Lollie turned to bestow upon her sister should have warned me. But thinking of Stephen, I took no note.

So far, Aunt Mellie had not asked about Stephen nor even mentioned him. Now she said abruptly, "Is that man gone?"

"No."

"I forbid you to see him! And you *will* obey."

"No, Aunt Mellie."

Her face suffused with anger, she slammed her cup to the saucer. "You defy me?"

"Yes, Aunt. I am not a child to be ordered about, I shall see whomever I wish whenever I wish. You don't *own* me. You may rant and rave all you like, but I shall do what I think best."

She seemed stunned, then rallied, eyes narrowing. "You will mind me, or—"

I couldn't let this go on any longer. I pushed back my chair and rose. "Aunt," I said gently for all at once in a rush, I knew how much, deep down, that I really loved her, "please try to see the situation with understanding. A man is hurt, he has to have a place to stay, to rest and get well. Is that so bad? He won't be in your way—"

"You may be sure of that!"

I shrugged. All the bitterness kept her from so much— all the tenderness, the gentleness she could have had. She was so tiny, so unbelievably explosive I had the strong urge to go to her and place my arms tight around her shoulders. Would she fight? Strike out? The moment passed, I watched her snatch up half a glass of wine and drink it off, then shove back her chair and leave the table, and the room, without another glance at me.

I might be furious at her, but I couldn't stay that way. One minute I wanted to stamp my foot and shout at her, the next minute I worried about her—whether she was getting sufficient rest, or eating as much as she should. Sometimes the trays came back from upstairs with the food scarcely touched. She was my charge, my concern, and, along with little Aunt Lollie, would be as long as they lived.

Narcisse had made soup—from rabbit, I suspected, but which still smelled heavenly—and hot corn biscuits. This, she said, would tempt a man's appetite. With it she packed apple pudding and as much hot coffee as Stephen could drink. Did I want to carry it?

Did I! I took no persuading. Jason would be on hand to help. The meal in a wicker basket over my arm, I made my way to the lean-to.

The room, such as it was, was low of ceiling, with a rough board floor and one tiny window; the furnishings a table, a chair, a stool, and a cot. Stephen lay flat, his face turned toward me. Now that I was here, I found myself suddenly hesitant.

He smiled ruefully. "Hello there. Sorry I can't get up for the amenities—seems I got myself in a bit of a fix, so I'm to be a guest for the next week or two." He gestured. "Whatever you have in that basket smells mighty good."

"Oh—yes." I shook my mind free of cobwebs and set down my burden, pulling a stool close to the bed. Jason was nowhere to be seen. "Do you want me to—I mean, can you— Well, eat by yourself, or—"

"I can, sure." He gingerly pulled himself up on his elbow, and I sprang to place pillows at his back. "Is that all right? Are you used to doing this—you've done it before?"

He nodded. "It's all right. As long as I don't move too fast or twist. These wrappings are tight and there's not much room left for breathing. But that's the general idea."

"Maybe they were put on a little too snug." Stephen wore a loose shirt open to the waist, and above the taut wrappings his naked skin showed. I tore my eyes away from the small pulse that beat at the base of his throat, remembering what I came for and that he was helpless. I reached for the basket, setting its contents carefully on the table. Narcisse had even included utensils.

"No, I can stand it. Best this way," Stephen replied, answering my remark, "for a while, anyhow. Jason knows what he's doing. He makes a pretty fine doctor, when all is said and done."

I'm glad for that, I thought, since there isn't a physician closer than Vancouver, a million miles away.

I dished up the soup, piled a plate with corn muffins, and saw Stephen eating before I sank to the low stool. The slight strangeness I'd felt at first was wearing away, and I was more at ease. "What happened?"

The Secrets of Montroth House   123

"My horse spooked—shied at something he heard in the brush—and got his feet tangled in the branches of an old windfall." Stephen paused and looked up. "He wasn't hurt, I was. That's the irony. The nag could at least have thrown me in the bushes and cushioned my fall." He'd been on his way north, he said. There was a logging camp at Silver Springs about forty miles from here that he'd wanted to look over for prospects.

On his way to somewhere north. Then he hadn't intended to see me, I hadn't entered into his plans. He wouldn't be here now if it wasn't for the accident. "More coffee?" I managed.

"Yes, if you don't mind."

Did it hurt him to sit up? Pity stung me. A big man, so strong—but in a while, too short a while, he'd be well again and gone. I poured, then wondered if I should leave. I was here, Stephen—the Stephen I'd dreamed about—was here, but there was something wrong. The talk was pleasant, but banal, almost as if he were making conversation just to fill in the time. There was a distance between us that had not been there before and it terrified me. I became aware of my hands twisting in my lap and sat up straighter, a smile on my lips.

"At least you will have two weeks of rest," I heard myself say politely, "then you can be on your way. Would you like more of anything?"

"No, I've about reached my limit. That cook is a jewel. You have some fine people here."

"I know that," I said quietly.

"And how are the aunts?"

"Both well, at the moment." I'd been staring at a picture tacked on the wall, a newspaper cut of some ducks on a pond surrounded by hills and trees. Jason had put it up, trying to beautify the room. On a small shelf, a dandelion was stuck in the neck of a bottle. He didn't pick the rhododendrons or azaleas, hadn't picked the daffodils, except those he gave me. Aunt Mellie didn't want the rhododendrons picked.

Tomorrow I'd bring a bouquet as big as my head of the last of the things and plunk it right here in the middle of the table.

"A penny for your thoughts."

"What?" I mustn't let him see how disappointed I was, and how hurt.

"You looked so far away, in deep thought. They keeping you busy?"

"Oh yes. I don't know why she thinks she should, but Narcisse is insisting I learn to cook."

For the first time I saw a grin break through, a real grin, and Stephen's eyes twinkled. "Well, a young lady can't learn too much of a good thing. The culinary arts can be pretty important—where would this world be if we had no sense of the combination of foods? Back chewing on bones and wearing our teeth down."

I laughed, happy to go along with him. "Around a smoky fire, and with skins dangling?"

"You have a vivid imagination. I like that. I seem to remember a sense of humor, too. One wet night you wished you'd worn waders."

I felt my cheeks grow pink. "It seems a long time ago."

"It wasn't. You bumped into me and knocked my stuff on the ground. That was the beginning."

Of what? I felt like crying, *of what?* His hand, big, wide, strong, lay on the blanket, a lock of that ink-black hair tumbled over his forehead. Men shaved every day, didn't they? Then Jason must have done it, since Stephen was clean-shaven. Where was Jason? It occurred to me that he might have purposely kept out of the way.

"Have you about finished in the library?" It was a casual question.

"N-no, and not for some time yet. But I've not been working at it so hard lately, either."

"Why is that?"

I hesitated. Stephen held out his cup and I set it back in the basket. "I don't really know. Well, I guess I do, too. I've been told there's no hurry, nor does there seem to be. There was to have been a sale, you see—at least that was my understanding, but nothing more has been said."

"They could have changed their minds."

"That's what I thought. But—"

I felt Stephen waiting. "But what?"

"Well—nothing. They don't get along too well some-times—with each other, that is. Of course," I added, "they're old, and notional."

"The library work could have been just an excuse to get you here."

"I'd like to think that," I agreed. I *had* thought it once, my mind corrected.

"Then if book work has fallen off, how do you fill your hours?"

I decided to be frank. There was no reason I shouldn't be, was there? "Actually, up until a day or so ago I was kept busy running after them. Then there was the scare with the séance."

"What scare?"

I explained, then said, "Aunt Lollie went into a decline and I was really concerned for her. We never did find out if it was a prowler or not. Then Aunt Mellie came down with a cold and was completely out of hand—Hessit, the maid, or I, had to be with her every minute." I remembered dancing attendance on ill-tempered Aunt Mellie, enduring her insults.

"But you—you've been all right?"

"No. If you want me to be honest—not quite. I must be accident-prone because I've fallen through a roof, very nearly had a flowerpot hit me, and tumbled down a flight of stairs in the dark."

Stephen's eyes had undergone a subtle change; he seemed to be weighing my words. "But you weren't hurt," he said then.

"Not seriously." I shook my head and rose. "Only a few bumps and bruises. I was lucky."

He'd had plenty of time to reach for my hand as he'd done before, but throughout the visit there'd been nothing like that. Why did I feel so far from him, as if I was being pushed away? Something else was in his thoughts, I knew it. Something I didn't understand, couldn't fathom. Tears were close behind my eyes, my eyelids burned. He hadn't touched me, or acted as if he wanted to, hadn't spoken warmly or with even a hint of depth. Oh, we'd laughed together and for a while were on the same footing as before, but it had ended in nothing.

I gathered up the dishes, replaced them in the basket. "Can I get you anything? Send Jason to you?"

"No, I'm fine. And Jason will be along. He deserves some freedom; he's been like a mother hen. And with his time taken up with me like this, Haines has had to fill in. I expect he had his hands pretty full before, with that pen of dogs. So far, I haven't heard them." Stephen pushed himself back carefully, and I reached for the pillows behind him. Lying prone again, he sighed. "Something mighty cramping about a situation like this. Thanks for what you did."

With the basket over my arm, I turned. "I'll come again."

"Do that. Lori—" Briefly his eyes held mine, then he turned his head on the pillow. "No—forget it."

My eyelids stung again. What had happened between us? Where was the vibrancy, the almost irresistible pull? Was it all mine, had I dreamed the other? I must have hoped too much, assumed too much.

♊ 12 ♊

I DIDN'T SEE STEPHEN again right away. I felt bruised, bewildered, and I needed time to think. His announcement had shocked me more than I would have thought possible, and I was puzzled and deeply wounded by his attitude. I'd been certain he was as attracted to me as I was to him. Why had he changed? Withdrawn? Had I made too much of a chance encounter? I thought when I took dinner to him he enjoyed my visit, yet he hadn't asked me to come back. I volunteered. I would go of course, there was nothing else I could do, and meet him on his own terms. I would hold up my head and be pleasant.

Concurrent with his arrival, the climate in the household worsened. I was already aware of Aunt Mellie's state of mind. Did Aunt Lollie know of the newcomer? How was she taking it? In defiance of stern orders, I presented myself at Aunt Lollie's door.

I knocked, and repeated the knock before a small choked voice answered. Once inside, I started forward in alarm. "Aunt Lollie, what is the matter?" But I knew. She'd heard. Or seen. And closeted herself in her rooms, fearful and trembling. The old lady's face was puckered and ash-white, her mouth worked as if she were about to burst into tears.

"Lorene, you will be the death of us yet! I said so, didn't I? Lorene, you must tell that man to leave immediately! Who is he, anyway? We did not invite him here! I looked out of my window and—"

I soothed her and explained the best I could. "Where is the bright, cheerful lady who came down to the dinner table," I asked, "the one so beautifully gowned in lace and lavender satin?"

If there was one appeal to Aunt Lollie, it was through her vanity. The little face smoothed and broke into smiles.

"I don't know why you're so upset," I said, "or why you don't want to meet him. Aunt Mellie either! He was just on his way somewhere else when the accident happened, that's all. For this period of time, he is confined to bed and must remain so."

"He won't bother us?"

"Bother you? Of course not! Not if you don't want him to. Why should he?"

She was like a child. Her hands fluttered. "But dear me, you don't know what a turn this gave me!" Aunt was trembling in her relief.

Unthinkable in this day and age that one could be such a recluse as to fall to pieces at the mere prospect of facing an outsider! It was on the tip of my tongue to clear up the issue of how they managed the other travelers to Montroth, but I decided I had better not. It would be sure to throw her into panic again.

"He will not trouble us further? And will leave and not come back?"

"Why should he stay?" The ragged edge of hurt in my voice was totally overlooked by Aunt Lollie.

"Well," she sighed, "I cannot expect you to understand our situation and why we must insist upon our way of life. Suffice it to say that we are old and set in our habits. I truly am sorry for my agitation, but you see we just can't have strangers poking about."

Can't? My mind caught on the word. Why couldn't they? I'd misinterpreted her meaning of course. It was only a figure of speech.

Work in the library occupied me for a time. I penned a note to Belinda for Jason to mail when next he drove out, ate my noonday meal alone, and later went to the kitchens. Narcisse was making pies, turning, rolling, shaping the dough into pans. She glanced over her shoulder, nodded briefly and lifted a floury hand, then returned to her pies.

I stepped to the back porch, my gaze drawn irresistibly to the lean-to. Was it only yesterday I'd seen Stephen? It must be tiresome, I thought, and lonely for him to lie still all day, lonely and tiresome and difficult. I had been thinking only of myself. Whatever my feelings, I should try to make his time easier. I would ask Narcisse to let me carry his dinner to him tonight; there would be, I thought wistfully, at least some contact, even if we only chatted like mere acquaintances as we'd done before.

The rhododendrons, spring-blooming plants, were on their way out, but by careful selection I could still manage the bouquet I'd vowed to bring.

The outdoors smelled good. I knelt, picking away dead leaves, cleaning up the last of winter's litter from beneath the branches when I heard a guttural cry. The next moment, Ana hurled herself into my arms.

"I ha'—I ha'—" she gurgled. The brown arm that wore the bracelet had a stranglehold around my neck.

"It's all right," I said. What was this all about? "It's all right—Ana, it's me, Lori! What are you afraid of? Nothing is going to hurt you. Come now, tell me what's wrong."

"I ha' pokit aroun' in them orchet an' I fin'—I fin'—"

"You find what?"

Her young-old face settled and went blank. "I dunno, I dunno. I feared!"

"No—no," I soothed, "you're all right. Don't cry any more." She smeared at the tears with a small fist, sobbing wildly against my shoulder, the convulsive tremors growing less as I patted her gently.

"Don't think about it any more," I said. "Whatever it was can't hurt you. You're safe. Nothing can hurt you. Shall we go together to the orchard and see what frightened you?"

"No! No!" The black head burrowed frantically into my shoulder. What in heaven's name *had* she seen?

"All right, we won't, then. But look—just look at the orchard. Even I can't see anything wrong there. Just sunshine, and trees, and birds, and blue sky up above. Blue sky everywhere. And in between, flowers and grass."

I had the girl's full attention now; the tight-clinging arms relaxed their hold as she peered up at me. She swiped at her eyes again.

"You know what? I'll tell you a secret—you're going to have a new dress. Did you know that? A pretty new dress all your own. It will be blue, and you can wear the yellow beads with it. How about that?" I looked up to find Jason watching us, a sympathetic smile on his face. He held out a wild daisy picked from the edge of the forest. I tucked it in Ana's hair, and she went off, pleased.

When I returned to the house, I did so by a circuitous route, thinking hard. What was amiss in the orchard? The girl had been terrified; she'd seen *something*. I'd looked myself, noting that here and there under the trees the earth was new-scratched, as though some creature had been digging, but saw nothing out of the way, nothing at all to send a girl screaming in abject terror. Could it have been some pocket of shadow at the edge of the forest, some hobgoblin creation of dark branches, a crouching figure made of a bush, perhaps? It wasn't likely that it was an animal; surely none were venturesome enough to come this close to the house in broad daylight. Besides, Ana would have recognized an animal. No, it had to be shadows which had startled her and set her off.

Narcisse was finished with the pies, three beautiful specimens stood on the counter waiting to be baked. "What was Ana after?" I demanded.

"Onions. We got onions out there."

"Give me a pan," I said, "I'll get them."

"No soil hands," Narcisse stated. "Narcisse get. Lori no worry, go on 'bout business now." She added grimly,

"Narcisse take care of. An' no worry 'bout Ana. All right?"

About to pose my request to take Stephen his dinner, I looked up to see Aunt Mellie in the doorway, gesturing imperiously. "I need help. Will you come at once? You should not be bothering Cook, anyway."

Which was it, that she needed help, or that she wanted to keep me away from the kitchens, which she considered beneath my dignity? At least her demand was couched in the form of a request. I followed her without comment.

It seemed the memoirs were not dead after all, and I was kept busy until dinnertime. She dined at the table that night, and even Aunt Lollie, in diaphanous purple and ecru lace, put in a brief appearance. Although on the edge of my chair lest an argument break out, all went well.

Talkative and pleasant, Aunt Mellie was a surprise. She dwelt at length upon subjects already discussed, but with a temper so genial I didn't mind, and I laid my disappointment at not seeing Stephen aside and entered freely into the conversation. If it were like this all the time, I thought, how nice living at Montroth would be!

When the issue of money came up, I edged away. Aunt was persistent. "Just a moment, Lorene! You don't seem to want to talk about it but I do. And let me remind you of one thing—I have made my will in your favor."

I groaned inwardly. "I don't want your money." I'd said the same thing many times before.

"Nevertheless, you have it."

"But you can't," I reiterated firmly. "What about your sister—what about Aunt Lollie?"

The old lady's laugh was short. "It isn't likely she'll outlive me, is it?"

"I don't know about that, but I won't change my mind on the matter. I know you don't have any other relatives, but how about some of your previous visitors to Montroth? You must have a favorite—one you particularly liked. Mr. Swanson or Mr. Owens, or even Werner Venson—you said he'd been here, and stayed the longest. He could be deserving, what about him?"

Aunt suddenly giggled, her eyes strange and opaque. "Oh, I don't think they're in much of a position to have opinions either way."

"Well," I said flatly, "I won't take it, and that's final. I don't need it and didn't come up here for any such thing. No, I'm quite well enough off as it is, thank you."

"Don't be so stiff-necked," Aunt Mellie snorted. "What's wrong with being a rich girl? And you don't get my *sister's* half; still, it amounts to thirty thousand pounds, give or take a bit. For fifty years that's lain safe in the Bank of England gathering interest—should be a bit more by now. And don't argue with me. It's done and you've nothing to say about it. All witnessed and proper."

It was a long hop from being on paper to being legal, especially up here, but I wasn't proposing to worry about that. I was relieved when Aunt pushed back her chair and announced she would retire.

By this time it was much too late for visiting Stephen. I, too, retreated to my quarters. It was ten o'clock, and the moon big and bright, a fair and lovely hour for a breath of fresh air. At seventy, one dozed with knees close to the fire or napped uneasily beneath the counterpane, but why should I be trapped in the house? The dogs had been quiet for several days and peace reigned everywhere. I put on my coat and went out.

Was Stephen asleep? I wondered. No lamp burned in the lean-to. Pity wrenched me. What was there for him to do except to eat and sleep? How I wished he were here with me now!

Moonlight silvered every path, touched every treetop in the forest, turning it into a magic fairyland of beauty. Even the old barn—Aunt Mellie called it the Mews—where Jason slept in his little room, was outlined in brightness. The big House was quiet, crowded by puddled shadows.

Over beyond the orchard, down in the woods and on the other side of the clearing where Jason cut logs, I caught the sleepy chirp of a bird, and another replied. Night wind touched my lips and turned them cool, and I tasted the freshness. The earth was soft and yielding underfoot, and I walked slowly around the great pile of the mansion and to the other side, toward the shrubbery.

Beyond was the small enclosure where I'd first seen Ana, and Belinda had called her back to the kitchens; the trees in the corner where the little scullery girl had hidden were inky-black, the enclosed expanse surrounded on three sides by grass made silver by the moon. Had something stirred in the dark hollow? Silly—silly, I chided myself, don't start with the imaginings.

I moved out and away from the shrubbery, following the path toward the orchard. Here, too, all was silvered by moonlight. The old apple trees were in full rich leaf and each twisty sentinel harbored beneath it its own patch of dappled shadow.

I don't know how long I stood before I became fully aware of the silence. It was heavy, unnatural; it came slowly and it had weight and body and substance and seemed to press in against me, stifling the senses. Something was moving out there—something in the shape and figure of a person in a dark cape, or long flowing robe. It had knelt, or was bending over, scratching at something on the ground, scratching at the earth or digging.

I stood frozen in a patch of moonlight, unable to move. At that moment the figure, whatever it was, looked up and directly at me, for I could see the white face glimmering, then it leaped to its feet and fled like a wraith through the trees and into the forest.

My feet were numb, welded to the earth, my arms limp. I stood staring at the spot, feeling as if all the blood had drained from my body, at the mercy of the darkness and every evil that prowled in it.

Then as though they had seen the figure too, a violent outcry suddenly burst from the dog pens. One howl rose to shatter the night, then another and another until the entire enclosure was alive; they were leaping frenziedly against the wire. It broke the spell for me; fear, wild, primitive, unreasoning fear, such as I'd never felt before, jerked me into motion and sent me flying to the house and up to my room.

I jumped into bed, tempted to burrow into my bedcovers like a three-year-old and there remain until the night righted itself. But, as always, somewhere in the confusion there was a thread of coolness and common sense that brought me back to sanity. I demonstrated this by sitting up under my eiderdown and hugging my knees to still their shaking. Stephen—what was he thinking? He must have been shocked awake but unable to leave his bed, able only to wonder at the cause of the uproar.

The fire in the fireplace had died down to coals and the room was toasty-warm. Outside the moon still shone brightly, but my heavy curtains were drawn tight, and every lamp in the place was turned up as high as it would go. There was a time, I told myself grimly, to be wasteful, to enjoy warmth and light.

I knew no answer to all of this. What *was* in that orchard? Ana's violent reaction stemmed from something she had seen in the daylight; what I saw was in moonlight. Man or woman I could not have told, but it was human—of that I was certain, and with a furtiveness that chilled my brain and turned my flesh cold. Then the creature ran, faded into the forest like some demon of the night.

I turned the bedside lamp higher but it was going dry. Determinedly, I got as large a candle as I could find and padded across the room, lit it from a log in the fireplace, and set it in the sconce. I'm a spendthrift, I told myself recklessly. Poor Jason, I thought, as I piled more fuel on the fire.

In the morning Hessit would clean and refill the oil lamps with her customary efficiency, but wearing no expression whatsoever. Aunt Mellie would complain about the noisy dogs. Aunt Lollie would float down from her scent and feathers long enough to shake her head and flutter her hands, and the House would go on as if nothing had happened.

But what about Hessit? She had ears; the pen of dogs exploding must have sounded to her as they did to me, as if all the hounds of Hades clamored to be loosed. I'd give a pretty penny to know Hessit's honest opinion. She must have one.

And the apparition I'd seen. It wasn't Jason—it was too agile for Jason. Nor Haines. I knew Haines retired very early and he was old, too, and had rheumatism.

Who, then? Hessit? The idea was absurd. From what I'd seen, the Jamaican woman lived half out of her wits with fright most of the time and would never in this world be caught out after dark. It wasn't Ana and it wasn't Narcisse. I gave up; I might have dreamed the whole thing.

I slid down under the quilts, drowsy in spite of myself, then suddenly jerked upright. It *could* have been Narcisse, in that flowing dark shroud. Or even Ana, sufficiently freed of fear that she'd braved the place. A household had to dispose of its unwanted refuse, that which could not be turned into suitable food for the dogs. Perhaps late with her chores, Ana had simply gone out and was burying the accumulations of the day. Glancing up she'd beheld me standing statuelike in the moonlight and been as frightened as I, and bolted into the forest. The dogs' uproar hadn't helped. But something was wrong with these deductions. Narcisse would not have run—would have had no reason to do so, and would Ana have been bold enough to go back to the place—*at night*—which had so terrified her before?

Which left Aunt Mellie and Aunt Lollie. Suppose one of them had taken to burying her money in the earth, at night, in secret. Farfetched? Maybe not. So the episode reduced itself to an old lady and her quixotic notions? Of the two, it would be Aunt Mellie.

The next morning I rose early and presented myself in the kitchen for breakfast. This time Narcisse smiled, her huge arms akimbo.

"I fix soup," she announced, "good marrow soup, wit' vegetable. Corn, peas, carrot. Onion. Old recipe, my gran'ma make it for me. Best to put meat on bones—Lori too skinny. Said it once, say it again. Make fat, nice. Round, huh? Plump like ptarmigan, young man like. You marry wit' him? Nice, nice! Plenty papoose. Nice. You eat now, huh? Narcisse fix."

I almost choked, and could feel my cheeks redden. Unbelievingly I eyed the steaming cauldron Narcisse had placed before me.

"I can't eat all this! Just a small bowl, please, not more than half this much. Narcisse, it looks—wonderful, but so much."

But the big woman had something in her head and wouldn't give up. "Get fat for young man," she repeated. "There spoon, there bowl. Dig in. He no like skinny, hear bones rattle."

"I think you're jumping to conclusions," I countered desperately, "or having a nightmare, because it's not that way at all."

"Lori not know everything," Narcisse announced complacently. "No worry. Now get it down. Good soup! Narcisse got pudding too. Fix just for Lori."

I appreciated the gesture, even if the motive was awry. Narcisse had Stephen in mind, and had put two and two together. Recalling the conspiratorial wink at my offer to carry Stephen's meals, I blushed into my soup. She'd returned to her chores, paying me no further attention. After the meal I got on with the purpose of my visit, following Ana to the porch where she was shelling green peas.

She looked up, smiling shyly. "Got new dress?"

"Not yet. Soon, though," I assured her. "Ana, I want to talk to you. Think hard then give your answers. Do you understand? And I don't want you to be frightened."

She was more animated now than I'd ever seen her. "*Hier soir?*" Ana repeated as I questioned her. "Las' night?" She paused, appeared to reflect. "*Non. Le* gar-bage? Jason, he do. *Les autres fois, moi. Oui.* Las' night, *non. C 'a se line dita.*"

"But most of the time, you do?"

"*Oui.*"

"And it is buried in the orchard?"

Ana's eyes opened wide. "Ah, no. *Mais non!*" She shook her head positively. "Place by woods. Ees buree in place near by beeg trees—*le foret, n'est-ce pas*? By beeg trees. Not orchet. Not no more."

It was a long speech for her, more coherent than usual, and I'd heard what I expected to hear. Yet someone had been surprised and scurried off into the shadows! I could remember my own fright and sympathize with Ana's. With a bit of spare time on my hands, I'd examine that orchard again, making certain, of course, that the survey was in full daylight.

I went back to the kitchen and stood at Narcisse's elbow while she made coffee. "I've seen something," I said, low-voiced, "and I want an explanation if you have one. You've been at Montroth a long time and know pretty much what goes on. Does somebody here bury money or valuables in the ground?"

"I no' know what nobody bury in ground!" Narcisse's tone was curt, so curt I looked at her in surprise. "Lori full of questions. No ask no more questions, huh? Coffee ready, you carry breakfast now, stop with questions. Go, talk nice to man. He mighty tired of flat on back all day and all night. Like see pretty girl, make talk, feel better."

"Did you hear the dogs?"

"Dam' dogs."

"I saw what they were barking at. Somebody was digging in the orchard. *What for?*"

"Damn!" the big woman exploded. "I no know nothing! I cook, I eat, sleep, mind own business. Now Lori be good girl, carry breakfast. Be sweet, put worry away. No can make good talk when all pucker with worry. I say Narcisse take care of, an' that so. You better believe! All right, go."

I went, saying no more. She was keeping her own counsel. If she knew anything—and I was convinced that she did— she wasn't telling.

"Just a minute," I said, and after obtaining a jar of water, hurriedly picked rhododendrons and made my way to the lean-to. Stephen was lying on the cot with his face turned to the wall. I set the jar quietly on the table and went back to the house.

"He's asleep!"

"Well, wake him! Man got to eat. Sleep too much anyhow. Wake him up. Here." Narcisse shoved the laden basket into my arms.

This time I paused on the threshold. I didn't know what to do—speak out, clear my throat, call his name?

He turned his head. "Oh! It's you." Did great warmth lurk in his eyes before the eyes' expression was masked? Was it tenderness I'd seen on his lips before he caught himself? I was more bewildered than ever.

"I hope you're hungry, because I brought breakfast. I guess Narcisse wants to build up your strength."

He eased himself up on one elbow and grinned. "Yeah, I think so too. From the size of the portions she's been sending, she must figure she has to haul me all the way back from death's door."

Jason wasn't in evidence now either, and I blessed him for it. Were my visits anticipated? "This is the fifth day," I said, carefully unloading the basket. "How do you feel?"

He grunted. "Like a caboose shunted onto a spur track. Actually, better. Jason seems to think the ribs are knitting fine."

"That's good news," I said but inwardly felt a pang. The time was going so fast! "Did he say when you could get up, walk around? Does he have any idea?" I'd filled a plate, added the bowl of steaming soup, and handed it over. Coffee, also steaming hot, was in the fat jug, and I poured a cup of it and set the cup at his elbow. Then I pulled the stool forward and sat down.

"The end of this week probably, if all goes well. It's good of you to do this." He gestured toward the red blossoms on the table. "And flowers too. You brought them."

"The first trip," I agreed. "I couldn't carry them, and the food, at the same time." Laughter bubbled up. "Aunt Mellie would skin me alive if she knew I'd picked her precious rhododendrons. It's the only thing on this whole place— outside the House, that is—that she's particular about." I'd felt terrible at her rejection when he'd needed help, and I still did, but hesitated to bring up the subject.

"What was the matter with the dogs last night?"

Again I hesitated, then said frankly, "There was something in the orchard, and you know how dogs are, one starts and they all join in."

Stephen took a swallow of his coffee; he seemed to be watching me, waiting for my answer. "What do you think it was?"

"Well—" I hedged, "Narcisse says there are a lot of animals around, sometimes even wolverines."

"Right. *Carcajou*. French-Canadian for Devil-Dog. But wolverines wouldn't come up this close, night or day. It had to be something else."

"Then I couldn't say." I rose, picked up the empty cup and refilled it. "I think Narcisse's coffee must be the best in the world," I said. "I never was much of a coffee-drinker—it was always tea—until I came up here." Stephen reached for the cup and our fingers met; it was as if a bolt of lightning whipped through me. Had he felt it too? He looked up at once, but his expression was inscrutable.

"Are you keeping busy?" The question was polite, casual, the sort one might ask of an afternoon drop-in.

"Quite. We went back to working on the memoirs again. Aunt Mellie is writing her memoirs, you know."

"And your other aunt?"

"Up in the clouds most of the time. Her gowns, perfumes, feathers, mark her days, but she's happy, poor old dear."

"By any chance, has either of them mentioned someone by the name of Swanson? He's the cousin of an acquaintance of mine. He left Vancouver and headed up this way, but never made it to where he was going. I just wondered if he'd stopped in passing."

I nodded. "Yes, a Mr. Swanson was one of the visitors to Montroth."

"How long was he here?"

"I don't know," I said, "but it must have been some time ago—three, four years at least. Was he something of a plant fancier? He was working on developing a new type of fertilizer, Aunt Mellie said. They turned the greenhouse over to him and he worked there."

"No, this man was a government surveyor, and more recent."

"Oh, then it must have been a different Swanson. That greenhouse hasn't been used for ages. I found his wallet in one of the plant trays; it was moldy and had been there for a very long time. There were no cards or anything, but the initials *S.S.* were stamped on the outside. What was the given name of the man you're talking about?"

"Sigurd. A Scandinavian fellow, and as I understand it, he knows this part of the country pretty well, so there was little likelihood of him getting lost."

No, I thought, there was no connection, there couldn't be. It wasn't the same man, not even the same name. Besides, the time was entirely different.

I reached for the plate, but Stephen shook his head. "I'm looking forward to getting some exercise," he said. "Would you be willing to show me around?"

I nodded, trying not to appear overeager.

He grimaced. "Have you seen Jason? To tell the truth, these bindings are so tight they're about to cut off the circulation. When Jason does something he believes in doing it up right. It wouldn't hurt to loosen them a bit."

I hesitated then said, "I haven't seen him, but I can try if you like." I but wondered at my temerity. "I've never done anything of the kind, but you can tell me how."

"Would you?" His dark eyes, so close, held mine. "Your hands are so small."

"But strong." Let's make this a businesslike experience, I told myself, thoroughly matter-of-fact. But it wasn't, not entirely.

He sat up, indicated where the strip of material ended, and I unwrapped it very carefully. My fingers, touching his skin, ached to linger. "Does that hurt?"

"No, just all at once it feels loose inside, like something wants to fall apart."

I was startled and drew back at once. "Oh! Then maybe I shouldn't be—"

"No, go ahead. You're doing fine."

My fingers tremble, I could have said. I'm so very afraid I'll hurt you, yet I want to touch you—your chest, your shoulders, your face.

Stephen took a shallow breath, then another, and grinned. "Back to myself again. Feels great."

I hadn't taken the binding off completely, just loosened it. When I commenced to rewrap, I tried to do it exactly the same as Jason had done, yet with a little less constriction than before.

"Is that all right?" I paused to evaluate my handiwork. "This is all new to me, and you'll have to say straight out what I should or shouldn't do. If the wrappings aren't on tight enough will the ribs still heal? Could my loosening them cause damage?"

"You worry too much. I'm fine. Lori—." I wasn't prepared for what came next; he caught my hands suddenly in both his own and carried them to his lips as a man impassioned.

My breath caught in my throat and no words would come. What did he want to say? This was a moment—but I was losing it. Then the time was gone, past, and I couldn't get it back. He loosed his hold and with a slight shrug and lift

of the brows, eased back on the pillows again. For a while
he didn't say anything.

"Stay and talk for a bit longer. Please?"

It was as if the other never happened. My throat felt tight,
I swallowed to relieve it. "I really should—"

"You don't have to go back right this minute, do you?"

"N-no, I guess not." I struggled for self-possession, and,
in a measure, felt coolness return. "What do you want to
talk about?"

"Anything and everything. What you do with your time,
how things are for you. What your plans are, after Montroth.
But you still don't mean to leave."

"No. I thought I would once, but I changed my mind. I
came here to be with them as long as they lived, and—I
guess that's about it. Even if things get really bad, I'll stay.

"I play cards with Aunt Lollie, dominoes, do puzzles
with her, and look at the photo albums she sets such store
by. She must have at least twenty of them and insists they
are hers, every one. I think she'd scratch her sister's eyes
out if Aunt Mellie tried to take any of them. They almost
came to blows once at the dinner table over some of those
pictures. It was just something to quarrel about. That was
when Aunt Mellie got sick on the wine. Then Aunt Lollie
managed to get her royal families all mixed up. I'm afraid
she was going backward instead of forward. Which is hardly surprising since both aunts live so far in the past."

"Are they senile?"

"Sometimes I think so, other times not. I just don't know.
I've never lived around anybody aged before."

"Why did they leave England?"

I said I didn't really know. They must have their own reasons, and both of them seemed to like it well enough here.
"Living so long together, though, and in such isolation," I
said, "they've developed some strange notions, and are very
set in their ways. Even as sisters they are not at all chari-
table toward each other and I almost think at times—"

"What?"

"Oh, nothing."

"No more accidents?"

It was said with a pointedness I couldn't miss, but I replied lightly, "No, no more accidents. I've been trying harder to keep out of my own way." I rose. "I've been going on and on, and it must all seem terribly trivial." I gathered up the breakfast things and packed them in the basket. "Sure there is nothing I can get for you before I leave?"

He shook his head. Again his eyes held mine, level and—what? Cool? Once more I couldn't read his expression. "I'm sorry if I've hurt you. You weren't frightened?"

"Of—?" I knew what he meant. "No. I wasn't frightened."

"Then will you be back?"

"Yes, to show you around."

Walking out, I wanted to cry. If I weep every time I come out here, I told myself, I shouldn't come again. But I knew I would.

ᴗᴗ 13 ᴗᴗ

I NEEDED SOMEONE TO TALK TO about my fears and to advise me. Why hadn't I spoken out frankly and freely to Stephen? Because I didn't know him as well as I thought I did. Maybe, I thought dismally, I didn't know him at all.

There was a certain secrecy about him, hidden places that resisted invasion and made a wall between us. He asked questions, but gave little of himself in return. Only once, for the one startling moment, had emotion broken through, but it was a lapse he'd instantly regretted for he'd quickly withdrawn. What was I to think? Surely he didn't want us to be any closer. Surely he wouldn't want to be burdened with my problems and fears.

No, I would keep my worries to myself, puzzle over them and work out the answers if I could. There had been no more touchy situations anyway, so far as I was concerned. I'd told Stephen that much.

At dinner that night Aunt Mellie demanded to know if I was seeing "that man."

Yes, I told her, I was seeing him.

"After you were expressly forbidden to do so?" She was beside herself with anger.

"Aunt Mellie, calm down or you'll make yourself ill! You've no right to insist upon such a thing. I've told you before, I am a grown woman, not a child, and I do as I please. Aunt, do understand. I care for you very much and want to get along, but I am *not* under your thumb nor answerable to you."

She wouldn't listen, wouldn't hear what I had to say, and marched from the room. I let her go. I hated these confrontations, I meant to be kind and considerate, but I wouldn't be pushed.

Aunt Lollie was always the most pleasant of the two, yet it was conniving little Aunt Lollie who insisted I visit her after dinner, because she wanted "to have Lorene all to myself," as she put it. I had long since learned that if one or the other of them gave me anything—beads, a belt, ribbon, a cheap stone ring, I was expected to wear it. Upon responding to Aunt Lollie's demand, I forgot to remove a ring Aunt Mellie had given me from my finger, and the old lady pounced on it immediately.

"Where did you get that?"

"Your—Aunt Mellie made me a gift of it," I said. "Isn't it pretty?"

"Pthah!" Aunt Lollie spat, her little face convulsing. "Something she wouldn't want and is ashamed of. Probably threw it away and dug it up again. Now when I give presents—"

"Please, no!" I insisted. "I don't want anything."

The old lady was rummaging feverishly in her jewel box and came up with a brooch. It looked old, a quaint piece with rubies and pearls set around a large cameo, in an elaborate gold mounting. "Dear Mama gave me this," Aunt Lollie said grimly, "and now it is yours." She reached to pin it to my collar. Another thing I'd learned was that protesting could be time wasted; it was better to accept, tender thanks, and await the opportunity to return the object.

She reached for a photo album and I almost refused to look at it with her. More and more of late she'd go off on her memory-excursions, emerging in a weepy state and expecting to be soothed. I was relieved when Hessit knocked on the door. It seemed Aunt Mellie wanted to see me right away, in her rooms. I dropped the brooch quietly into the jewel case as I went out. These visits to Aunt Lollie were becoming increasingly wearing, and I heartily welcomed the interruption. Hessit, though, seemed alerted to some kind of unpleasantness, and there was a look of warning in her eyes. She paused in the hall as if endeavoring to put that communication across, then moved on.

When I saw Aunt I was shocked and appalled. I'd never seen her like this! The old lady had been burning something in the fireplace; its stench pervaded the room. But it was Aunt Mellie herself who caused my consternation. Her hair hadn't been combed. It stuck out in stiff wisps all over her head and hung over her forehead. Her eyes peered through the gray shock with maniacal intensity.

She came at me, claws set. "You have been neglecting me!" she screamed. But even as I shrank away in alarm, the wildness began to fade and normalcy return. The trembling fist clutching the old maroon sweater at her throat loosed its hold. I saw she was near collapse and leaped forward to catch her. Hessit was nowhere in sight, I'd have to do this alone. Had Aunt been tippling the blackberry wine again? No, it wasn't that.

"Here, come sit down," I urged. "I'll bring you a chair—" But the old lady struck my hand away sharply.

"I'm quite able to do for myself!" she snapped. "I do not wish to be coddled—I cannot abide coddling! I am not like my sister, always fawning about and demanding, demanding, demanding! I can take care of myself. I am not Letitia, crying at every bellyache." She sank weakly to the chair, breathing hard. "I say, where have you been? Don't tell me, I know. Have you no thought for anyone else, or is it that she refuses to let you alone? Yes, that must be it. You are not a selfish girl, nor are you partisan."

"But I've come," I managed, "every single time you've asked me!"

Aunt went on as if she hadn't heard. "You are the only sane one around this place," she said, "and you are not to sit lollygagging hours on end in my sister's rooms. I won't have it! And where were you last night when I needed you? Playing cards in my sister's suite, I'll be bound. What does she say to get you to run to her so readily?" Aunt moved her head petulantly, in an odd, side-to-side rocking motion. "I've been cold, and you didn't fix the fire. It is cold in here now! I called Hessit and she didn't come either."

Since the room was warm and would have been very pleasantly comfortable had it not been for that horrible smell, I was at a loss to understand the complaint. I tried to interrupt the whining tirade, and failed.

"What is the matter with everybody in this House? It is my House, is it not? Take care you answer immediately when you are summoned, young Miss, or you may find yourself out on the street." She peered at me intently through the dangling gray strands of hair. "But you wouldn't leave me," she whimpered, "would you? You said you were, once. You didn't mean it? I couldn't have that." A sudden look of cunning came over her, tightening her face, narrowing her eyes. "I had rather see you— Hand me that shawl— I'm *cold*."

Was this the same person I'd talked to, sanely and rationally, only this morning? Had Aunt's mind snapped? I shivered, but tried not to show the distress I felt. "Is there something in particular you want, or that I can do for you?"

Then under my very eyes the cunning faded, the old lady's features relaxed, and she smiled and made a futile dab at her hair. "I must look a sight," she said in a completely normal tone of voice. "My hair has been let go much too long. Send Hessit to me when you go out, will you? I want it combed at once. How can she be so neglectful! And you needn't do anything for me," she added cheerfully and without a trace of ill-feeling, "not at the moment. Only come when I ask. You may look in on me again later if you like. And you can go now."

She seized a poker and began jabbing at the blackening mess in the fireplace, coaxing it to burn.

"Would you like me to put another piece on the fire before I leave?" I offered. "I'd be glad to and it won't take a minute—"

Sharply, ruthlessly she whirled on me. "No, I wouldn't—! Now get out of here, you—you—"

I fled, but not before the log had fallen apart. Soot and ash flared up, and I saw what was smoldering—a woolen cape, a dark voluminous garment like the creature had worn in the orchard—

I was shaken and angry, physically sick. I won't go in there again, I told myself flatly. She can yell until she's hoarse. I'm sorry for her, very sorry because there seems something preying on her mind, but I won't go where I should have to defend myself. Something evil and dangerous lurked there, something callous and witchlike that could smile and turn a knife at the same time.

I once thought it could be Aunt Lollie, enveloped in the disguising robe, who prowled by moonlight. I should have known better. With her frills and foibles, her scents and bonbons, little Aunt Lollie at her best was sweet vacuity; at her worst, sly and vindictive. But she hadn't been out-of-doors in all the years she'd been at Montroth, and she quivered at a breeze.

So it was Aunt Mellie in the orchard. What was she doing there? I couldn't overlook the fact that she might have been burying some valuable to secrete it from her sister. But the sudden changes, just now, in her rooms made me wonder if she was demented. Just how far would she go? I'd long suspected her subject to spells, but could I believe her capable of actual attack?

I felt as if a net were around me, drawing tighter, drawing around all of us, as if something horrible were looming and nothing could be done to stop it.

Wearily, I welcomed a break. Hessit had managed to finish one of Ana's dresses. I was well enough versed in fancy stitchery, but would never have tackled anything like this. She'd done a beautiful job; the dress was simple, attractive and wholly suitable. Excitement should have loosed Ana's tongue; the effect was just the opposite, but sparkling smiles bridged the gap. A little girl was miraculously elevated to the status of young lady.

Narcisse offered tea and I refused. She eyed me, frowning. "Trouble?"

I nodded. I was too tired to quibble. Jason had taken Stephen's meal; they hadn't thought I was coming. It was late, anyway.

"Dem two crazy ol' lady. Dey kill each other yet."

"No, it wasn't that. But I'm sick of it. In our own way, we're all terrorized. Well, I'm going to put an end to it."

Narcisse looked startled. "What you goin' do?"

"What I should have done a long time ago. Take charge." But I'd had enough of the subject. "How is Stephen—Mr. Landrau?"

"He all right. Jason wants he stay in bed 'nother two, three days though. Better be sure. Got rest of life to get up, walk 'round. Take time to get better, that good. You carry food tomorrow, huh? Think man miss be wit' pretty girl. Ask where is she? Narcisse feel like say, fight wit' crazy ol' lady so not come. By-an'-by come for sure."

"Narcisse," I said abruptly, "why don't you leave here? Why do you stay? Why don't you go to some safe place and take Ana with you? It won't get better; it can only get worse."

She shrugged her big shoulders and didn't meet my eyes. "Narcisse no go. What for leave? No talk no more either. All talked out. Got work to do now." It was always the same. When she didn't want to talk, she didn't: "Lori no worry no more anyhow. Ever'thing be fine. A'right?"

Bed that night felt very good. It had been a long and worrisome day, and I was exhausted. It seemed I had barely fallen asleep before I woke—or something woke me. I lay listening, all my senses sharpened to the source of that disturbance. But everything was still, the stillness of death.

Bright moonlight lay in a silver bar across my bed and across the floor to the far wall. Suddenly I froze, my ears straining. Was there someone out in the hallway, moving toward the stairs? I thought I heard the slither of a footstep followed by the faint creak of a loose protesting board. No, it was closer to the landing, it was not directly outside. I pushed back the coverlet and got out of bed, my heart thumping, and made my way across the floor to lay my ear against the door.

For what seemed an eternity there was nothing, no sound and no movement at all. The silence was utter and complete. I straightened in relief; there was nothing more. I glanced back to the cozy nest I had just left, the soft eiderdown and plumped fat pillows beckoning me. Whatever it was, had gone anyway. In the act of turning back to bed, I heard it again—a sharp bump and scrape as if someone were moving furniture about, or as if a door—or a drawer—were being opened and closed. It seemed to come from downstairs.

Aunt Mellie—could it be Aunt Mellie? Suppose she had wakened and was in another of her spells and would harm someone? Hessit was with her, but maybe Hessit had fallen asleep. These past few days had taken their toll of her, too. And if Aunt Mellie were in a mood like that of earlier today, what harm could she *not* do? I ran my tongue over my lips, for they were dry. I swallowed hard for my throat was dry too. Then I turned and swiftly snatched a blanket from the bed.

The door made no sound as I opened it. Moonlight streaming through the narrow oriel windows at the end of the hallway cast an unearthly glow on the ancient carpet, but beyond, the head of the stairs lay in clotted shadows, the long stretch of steps leading downward, descending into complete blackness.

Cold perspiration damped my palms as I clutched my blanket and moved toward the head of those stairs, frighteningly aware that I made a glowing silhouette to anyone posted below. But no one stopped me; no voice spoke out; the silence was the silence of the Beyond. Who was ahead of me? Who would be moving stealthily through the house at night but Aunt

Mellie? Not Aunt Lollie, Aunt Lollie was afraid of her own shadow.

I gained the bottom of the stairs at last and melted into the blackness. Then I caught, off to my left, the scrape of a foot against carpet. There—there it came again. My heart banging in my throat, I advanced with my blanket held before me. The next minute some object came flying, and I'd become tangled with a fighting, snarling fury, the small, brittle legs flailing, the vicious claws reaching for my head, my face. I knew of a certainty who I held now, and was shocked. My superior strength quickly won, and I had the little figure trapped, panting and whimpering its rage within the blanket.

The commotion brought Hessit and Narcisse. Somebody made a light. The angry figure scratched its way out of the imprisoning wrap, and Aunt Lollie stood up, panting and glaring at us all. Wispy white hair made frowsy strings down her back; her maribou wrap was torn half off her body and she'd lost her slippers. She looked around at the accusing faces and suddenly crumpled. "I want to go to bed," she whined.

I thought fast. There weren't many hiding places in this room. I turned quickly to rummage in the sideboard, and from the top drawer, behind a pile of linen napkins I extracted several twists of paper filled with powder. "Death comes to all soon enough," I said, for I understood all too well now, what was going on. "You couldn't wait, could you? You had to do it yourself—had to try again. What are you made of, anyway?" But I was talking to fluff—sniffling, abject fluff—and I turned away in disgust.

"Sometheengs else you lose? Find it rolled back by the wall," Narcisse said and held out a vial half full of the same fine powder. Aunt Lollie snatched for it but Narcisse pulled it back. "Oh no, guess not," she grunted. "I think not play funny stuff no more, huh?"

I wish I could believe that, I thought, I just wish I could believe it. "Get back up those stairs and to bed," I said to Aunt Lollie, "and right now!"

"But I—I can't—"

"You got down them when there was something you wanted badly enough, you can get back up them. Or would you rather I carried you?"

Mumbling angrily, she climbed the stairs.

14

Was it some stupid, mindless game they were playing? Did they hate each other so passionately one delighted to see the other suffer?

Poison—so that was it. I'd been blind. Aunt Lollie's bonbons, the weakness, the cramps. But why hadn't it killed her? Because Aunt Mellie hadn't wanted it to, hadn't given her enough, only doled it out with a sparse hand. She'd merely wanted to see her sister in trouble, to make her suffer, not to put her out for good. And the wine—had something been slipped into it by gentle little Aunt Lollie? And Aunt Lollie's upsets. Her "My dear, I always recover but in case one of these times I do not," meant something to me now. This must have been going on for years. No wonder they didn't want me, hadn't willingly sent for me! Two sisters practicing their nefarious rites upon each other— how had it all started? Aunt Lollie hinted at trouble back in England. Vaguely I recalled hearing of some accident—this when I was small—wherein Aunt Lollie had been thrown from her carriage when it collided with another vehicle on a Sunday drive. Aunt was not injured and even my father attached no significance to it. But such a mishap might have loomed very large to a little old lady. Going one step further I asked myself, was the fall from the carriage more serious than anyone thought? I remembered how angry Aunt Mellie became when I mentioned her sister's accident. Could there have been signs of mental deterioration as a result of that accident? Aunt Mellie was proud, she would have hated public exposure. Had she taken her sister and fled to the wilderness of Canada, and anonymity? Over the years, deterioration must have set in for both of them.

There were times, despite my assertion otherwise, when I would have left Montroth. Trappers, woodsmen, others—had done it. Visitors to Montroth had found their way in, I could find my way out. But how could I abandon my duty? I'd taken on the job of watching over two semi-demented old ladies, dangerous to themselves and obviously to anyone within reach. After my first revulsion, I knew I must continue to treat them the same as before. But *poison*?

I had been away from Stephen too long, and he had asked for me the next day. That in itself was warming. I left Aunt Mellie deep in a nap, Aunt Lollie cozy with Sir Basil, and descended to the kitchens. Narcisse had everything ready and was expecting me.

I carried Stephen's midday meal and found him propped up with pillows and watching the door.

At first he didn't say anything. I entered, unloaded the basket, filled his plate and cup, placed knife, fork, and spoon within reach, and sat down.

"You're not a mirage," he said at last, a wry grin taking the last of the somberness away. "Thanks for coming."

"My pleasure." I sat stiffly, hands clasped in my lap. He stared at me, then shrugged. "What's been happening? I'm a lot of use, lying here. But good news. Jason has revised his opinion. I can get up tomorrow. Has something gone wrong?"

I shook my head. "You're very observant, but no, not really. Sometimes I just get worried, that's all, and it's hard to throw off. Do you want the little household chit-chat, or do we talk politics?"

"Lori. Don't."

I looked down at my hands; my eyes swam with tears. Why did this have to be so difficult? I almost wished he hadn't come to Montroth at all, or that at least I could be honest with him. I made a tremendous effort and was more myself. I summoned a smile.

"Sorry, I didn't mean to be brittle. I hate sharp talk and never do it—or almost never. It's just that—well—things haven't been too pleasant lately."

I saw Stephen go grim, his jaw set. "You can leave."

"Do you actually think I would?"

He had no answer for that; or at least not one he could give. "Narcisse is quite a personality," he said at last. "She came out and talked for a while. If you turn your head I'll get up. I'm damned tired of lying around doing nothing, and there's no reason why—"

"No—don't!" I was instantly at his side, my hands on his shoulders restraining him. "You can wait one more day, then if Jason thinks it's safe, it's safe."

He relaxed, gave a lopsided smile. "All right. Can you be here for my first excursion?"

I nodded and rose. "I can," I agreed, "but I should go now. I don't want to leave them too long. You haven't even begun on your food. Don't worry about the things; someone can pick them up later." This time I just left— there was no goodbye—but I'd bring his meal tomorrow and go outside with him in the afternoon.

There had been no time lately for the library, work with books almost a thing of the past. The precious volumes lay where I left them, those on some of the shelves carefully sorted and in place, others remaining in jumbled disarray. I had managed to calm my thoughts somewhat, and it was restful here. I lost myself in my work. Later Hessit came to light the lamps, thoughtfully bringing a tray and returning still later to remove it.

She gestured, asking if there was anything I wanted. I said no, that I'd work a bit longer then read a while. She nodded and withdrew.

The House was quiet, peacefully sleeping. Tomorrow I would see Stephen again, but I should be more cheerful. It was hard not to speak of what was on my mind, hard not to show how I felt about him. Continued association might still melt the distance between us. I loved him so!

The book couldn't hold me. I leaned my head against the back of the chair and closed my eyes, worry returning. I should have realized sooner what was going on. Only skill that came of long practice allowed them to measure out the exact amount of poison. Just once, through carelessness or failing judgment, one of them would have died. It was a miracle both were still alive.

Even as I told myself this I heard the scream, thin, rising to unbelievable heights then choked off in a horrible gurgle. I leaped up as the dogs began to clamor, shoving a chair aside as I ran.

The sound, inhuman from a human throat, rose shrilly again—it seemed to be moving, it was coming toward the house! I heard Aunt Lollie at the head of the stairs and her quavery voice whimpering, "What is the matter—oh, what is wrong? Lorene—?" and the small thud of her body as she fell in a faint. I didn't stop.

I met Jason at the back door; all of us met Jason at the back door. He was carrying something which appeared to be a bundle of rags, but Aunt Mellie's grizzled head poked out of the end of it. Her wizened face was puckered and greenish, her eyes closed. There was a gash across her forehead and blood streaked her face.

I gasped. "Is she—dead?"

Narcisse had crowded in. She was taking charge, bellowing for us to go on about our business. Ana cowered in a corner; Narcisse pointed and the girl vanished. "No! Jus' bump. No die." She bared her teeth. "Narcisse fix. Damn!" she snarled savagely under her breath. "Help Narcisse get her up here."

Instead of obeying, Jason stood stiffly, his legs planted like trees, his great arms clutching his burden. Finally, he stepped forward and very deliberately dumped the bundle in a heap on the floor. Then still with that strange brilliance in his eyes, turned and walked out.

After seeing Aunt Mellie confined to her bed with Hessit set to watch over her, I went upstairs and revived Aunt Lollie. I told her I didn't know exactly what had happened, but it seemed Aunt Mellie had fallen and hurt herself.

Aunt Lollie sniffed and observed tartly that if Millicent was stupid enough not to know her way around by now, she deserved to hurt herself. She asked how badly her sister was injured. I detected a ghoulish note and closed off on the questions at once. I played one game of dominoes with her, noted she looked tired, suggested a rest, and sat with her until she drifted off. Before leaving the room I stood a moment looking down at the fragile little creature. Curls, lace, perfume, and shy laughter—sweetness personified. I shuddered. What possessed these two old women? The inflicting of pain, fine-drawn torture for each other, the anticipation and enjoyment of it, kept them alive. It was heinous, incredible.

As far as Aunt Mellie's accident was concerned, I had my own ideas. Aunt Mellie had prowled before. I thought Jason might have interrupted her and she'd struggled, injuring herself in the process. And Jason hadn't forgotten. Bringing Stephen in, he'd expected charity; faced with cold rebuff, he'd known shock, disbelief and outrage. No, I was not surprised at Jason's action. Was Aunt Mellie's nocturnal activity due to the restless prompting of a fevered brain, or did she have something buried?

There was one place I could go for an answer, and this time I was blunt. "Exactly what happened with Aunt Mellie?"

"She fall, hit head. Leetle bit harder, be one ol' lady, not two. Then no fight no more. She be all right."

"Yes, she'll be all right. But this business is not over yet. Can't you see what's happening? This place is falling to pieces. Crumbling. And so fast! I'm no good cook, but I can keep food on the table somehow. Narcisse, you've got to leave! There's no need for you to be involved in this."

"What 'bout man?"

"Mr. Landrau? He'll go, as soon as he can. A few days and he'll be gone. He has business elsewhere; he won't stay here." Narcisse looked at me oddly, I thought, but offered no comment. How could I make her understand that so long as she remained at Montroth there was danger for her? "Take Ana with you," I insisted, "and Hessit. Leave quickly."

But I was talking to stone, a sphinx with arms crossed. "No go. Where go to? This good place. Narcisse stay, Lori stay. No let harm come to. Jason watch, Haines watch. Hessit, she watch. Hessit good woman! Long time now tell Hessit put poison in mints, she no do. Narcisse maybe put poison in soup, better."

"You—knew?"

The Indian woman spread her hands, her voice growing harsh. "Narcisse guess. Ol' lady try kill each othair. One day make it maybe." She shrugged. "Narcisse hope! Then we stay here, have home, no bother be 'fraid. You savvy now I guess?" Narcisse darkly suggested that Jason and Haines had to stay in the woods, had to hide. When I asked her how long, Narcisse grimly replied, until they die.

My thoughts raced. I'd seen Jason in his moment, a man transformed by cold rage. Had Aunt Mellie some hold over him? Was that the reason he stayed? If it were true of Jason, how about the others? Gathering the unfortunates around them—and both old ladies must be equally guilty—wasn't philanthropy on their part, or kindness, they were *using* these people. Had they something on Haines too? Narcisse, and of course Ana, had no place else to go. Narcisse, I knew, earned her keep, and that of the little stray, ten times over, but in money matters Narcisse was totally ignorant. She wouldn't know how much she was worth or clamor for the wages honorably due her; she had a roof over her head, food and a bed and that's all she cared about. In spite of her strength and assertiveness Narcisse was not ambitious and would be lost in the outside world. Had the two old ladies cannily picked the jail cells, or worse, for their unpaid labor? It was entirely possible that Jason had killed someone and escaped with Aunt Mellie and Aunt Lollie when they left the country—the price of their freedom, turning his back on England forever.

"Haines?" I said slowly. I couldn't believe anything violent of him.

"No. He go to crazy-house. Die there."

Narcisse was right. Whatever the old man had or hadn't done, it was too late to make changes now. Haines' sentence would be an institution. Hessit, I didn't know. It could be as Aunt Mellie said, that the unfortunate woman had run afoul of a tribal taboo and been punished for it by having her tongue removed. Hessit had pride and she worked like a slave—she was *worked* like a slave, but she had once been a beautiful woman. Housemaids' positions would have been difficult for her to come by under the circumstances, and it seemed likely that the Misses Montroth, on the alert to their own advantage, had capitalized on her situation too.

The Indian woman rose, turned her back and began washing dishes. For her the conversation was finished. "Narcisse," I said and waited until she faced me. "What— is—in—that—orchard?"

She dropped a bowl with a crash. "I got clean that up," she said, touching the mess with her foot. "Good bowl, too. Only one like. No get 'nother so fine. Sorry 'bout that. You go now. Narcisse no want talk."

I said sternly, "The same song, sung the same way. You don't want talk. Well, I do! And I'd like an answer to my question."

Narcisse pulled a chair forward and sat down heavily. She was suddenly an old, old woman. "Narcisse know Lori goin' ask, but what can say? No even like talk 'bout it." She glanced nervously toward the door. "Narcisse only know 'fraid. Sometheengs evil—*n'ant ke suiskan alat*! Child of the Evil One. Make bad medicine, bad smell. How Narcisse, big woman, powerful, how she be 'fraid like leetle child? *Pesan taklat usoolin coli*—no! Of no theeng human is Narcisse fear, no man on whole eart'. But sometheengs else, no can fight, no can hit, no can holler at? No! Ghost walk, Narcisse see, one time then no more. One time plenty."

"But what is it?" I demanded. "What did you see?"

"Narcisse don' know! No argue wit' Evil-Who-Walks! Go garden, that close enough."

Yes, there was the orchard, and there was the garden. The garden was all right, onions, potatoes, carrots, peas grew there. But the orchard—

"Lori wonder in head, all time wonder. Aha, yes, Narcisse understan'. Now that all. Lori no ask no more questions! No talk 'bout *that* no more. Sorry, Narcisse no help. Lori good girl, let bads alone. All clear up, now we be happy again. All right?"

I was baffled. I stared at the big woman. She'd spoken of the poison, the people here at Montroth, but this was something else, something different. One thing was certain; she was deeply frightened. Of what, I still didn't know. It smacked of black magic. I'd felt the fear myself, the unreasoning terror that came from the dark unknown, and knew what she meant.

It was still early and I felt the need to calm my nerves. Returning to the library I chose a book, but on the stairs, met Hessit. She said Aunt Mellie was awake and wanted to see me.

Aunt was not only awake, but pleasant, and merely craved to be entertained. As long as she was like this, I would do my best to make her happy. I laid aside my book and recounted events and happenings in England that I thought would interest her, especially the activites of the royal family, so far as I remembered them. The old lady was in a nostalgic mood.

"You will be a rich girl when I die. After the estate is settled I expect you'll return to England, won't you? To Sussex, to your old home, perhaps?"

"Oh, I don't know." I wanted to avoid the question. Now Stephen and I were at least in the same country. Perhaps one day he might—"Canada is pretty nice, too."

Aunt sighed; she moved restlessly, her tiny fingernails scratched at the coverlet. "You mean you'd stay at Montroth? Don't forget all in the tower room is yours, also."

I'd been taken to the tower room, a cubbyhole scarcely larger than a closet, and shown dusty documents that I was not allowed to examine, which, she said, contained proof of the Montroth holdings.

"Well," she continued, "I suppose you could remain here, at that. My sister—" her voice rose, grew sharp, "my *dear* sister having left you her money too." The nails scratched harder. Abruptly she flung back the coverlet and shot bolt upright in bed. "I'm getting out of here. Hand me my robe!"

I was first shocked, then thoroughly out of patience. Why, she couldn't even stand! She was as weak as a reed, and only hours had passed since the knock on the head.

Suddenly I towered over her. "You lie down in that bed right now, do you hear?" Full of venom or no, this little wisp and bone had about as much weight as a beetle with its wings clipped. "Now you stay right there, do you understand? We've had enough of this foolishness. Even if you don't know what's best for you, I do. Look at your bandage— half off! Here, I'll fix it. Now do you want me to ring for Hessit and some cocoa? Or do you want me to leave and let you go on your rampage all by yourself? Make up your mind! One thing, if I do go, it will be a cold day before I come back. I'm not going to stand around and listen to any more of your tantrums. And you'll stay in this bed if I have to tie you to it!"

The old lady glared at me, but my outburst accomplished the desired result. She wilted, making a feeble attempt to adjust her nightcap which had fallen askew.

"Cocoa, then." She made a wry face, since it was wine she'd want, of course.

An hour later I left her, full of cocoa and good will and sleeping peacefully. I let myself out, posting Hessit to watch over her.

I'd had enough for one day. But as I was heading for my suite, Aunt Lollie called, "Oh, I'm so glad I caught you!" She beckoned me inside. "Have you been visiting my dear sister?" she purred. "How nice!"

I looked around. No inlaid mother-of-pearl table, no crystal ball? No Sir Basil. A half-emptied bottle of brandy stood on the sideboard.

"As you can see, I have been enjoying my photographs"— she gestured to an album open on the desk—"but it is so late I'll not ask you to go into them with me tonight. My mother always used to tell me that one captured the day with a picture, otherwise it was gone forever. A very astute observation, don't you think? Lorene my dear, I have something for you. Now don't say no! You are such a good girl and do work so hard for us that I feel you must have this." She pressed a framed photo into my hands. "My dear, my father and mother in a family portrait—my sister is there to the left, and myself next to my mother. Isn't that sweet?"

I wanted to believe the gesture was sincere, and that there was no ulterior motive. "Why, thank you very much. I know I shall cherish it. And now if there is nothing else—"

"Well, yes. Actually there is." She sighed. "You are a very good girl, Lorene, and I feel I can trust you. And because I feel I can trust you, I wish to ask you something. How is my sister, my poor dear sister? Truly now? Is she recovering satisfactorily from her accident?"

"She's a little—shall we say—squeamish yet, I'm afraid," I replied with some reticence, "but very much on the mend."

Aunt rubbed her little hands together with a dry, rasping sound. "Ah, I would have thought so!" she said brightly. "Nevertheless I would like to do what I can to speed her full recovery. I have here some of our Montroth special brandy—very choice, you understand—which I wish you to give to her." She handed me the bottle before I could protest.

When I left my arms were full of brandy and photograph. The last thing Aunt Mellie needed right now was alcohol, and I paused long enough to pour the brandy in the rubber plant down the hall. I placed the picture in its silver frame on my dressing table then looked at it, marveling. Aunt Millicent and Aunt Letitia, two cute little tykes all golden curls and sweet angelic faces, well-bred, well-cared-for children. What, I wondered again, had happened to bring about such a terrible change? They were normal when I knew them as maiden ladies, a bit eccentric perhaps, but normal.

I decided there was only one way to stop them, move swiftly to search out and destroy the poison, the little tucked away twists of paper, the small hidden vials, and hope that was all of it.

✆ 15 ✆

"HOW DO YOU FEEL?" I said when I saw Stephen the next morning. I emptied the basket, dished and poured. He ate with good relish then pushed his plate aside.

"Great!" He stood up, straightened to his full height, and grinned. I'd forgotten how tall he was, and looking at him my heart turned over, very slowly, in my breast. How I wanted his touch, his love! I turned away quickly, making some inane remark.

We walked a distance down the driveway and he pointed out where his horse had thrown him. Then we turned back back and slowly walked around the house to the small garden and the bench where we sat when he first visited Montroth. All week it had been unseasonably hot, a low, oppressive heat, and the earth was very dry. Branches on the big trees at the edge of the clearing drooped low, and a strong, resinous odor hung heavy on the still air.

Stephen walked along beside me, matching his steps to mine. His stride was free and easy. He had been looking at the forest and presently said, "The Cree would call this *aka le-ot ami*—fighting weather when tempers flare, or It-Speaks-Of Rain. The old men get together and nod when smoke from the fires rises in a straight line. The rain will hold off for a while, though."

"Do you know the Cree Indians?"

"I've met a few in my travels. They're nice people."

We surprised Jason by showing up almost at his elbow. He was pleased at our appearance and in his own fashion, greeted us. His thin blue shirt was stuck to his back with perspiration, and his grizzled hair was plastered to his head. Walking away Stephen said, "He handles those heavy blocks like a veteran, but it's too hard for him. At his age it seems he'd be better off someplace where he could take it a little easier."

"That's what I told Narcisse," I replied.

My companion paused, then asked, "What did she say?"

It was my turn to hesitate. "Well—she evaded the issue, as much as told me it was Jason's choice." I looked up at Stephen. "Where now?"

We'd halted; instead of answering his gaze explored my face, lingering on my lips then returning to look deeply into my eyes. Again that sharp, remembered awareness flared. I averted my head, feeling heat suffuse my body. Stephen cleared his throat and said huskily, "Where do you want to go?"

"You're not tired?" I asked, formal words to bridge an unsettling moment. I was still trembling—trembling with joy for I knew now that what was once between us was not dead.

"No, not tired at all. Don't worry, I'm fine. I noticed it was pretty quiet around here last night. No dog-music. I've heard them, now can we see them?"

I nodded. We followed the path around the shrubbery and to the pens. "Hi, fellows," Stephen called, and every one of the dogs crowded to the fence wagging their tails. "I thought you said they were vicious," he said to me.

"They were *supposed* to be vicious," I said, "that's what I was told. Both my aunts are frightened to death of them, Aunt Mellie especially. She's terrified. Superstitious, I think, in her way as bad as Narcisse."

"Did you say somebody left them here?" Stephen reached through the fence, scratching the dogs' chins and ears. Haines watched, beaming.

"A visitor to Montroth," I explained. "But I don't remember exactly who—Owens, I think, one of them was—a Mr. Owens."

Stephen got to his feet. "They're nice looking animals, mixed breeds, most of them, but all alert and in good shape. I should think anybody who could take care of dogs would want to keep them. It makes you wonder why Owens didn't come back after them." He raised his hand to Haines, the man eagerly returning his greeting, and we left.

"You'll be leaving soon, won't you?" I said, swallowing down the disappointment threading through me.

"I suppose so, yes. Or they'll be wondering what became of me, too. Funny about Swanson, just vanishing clear off the earth. You mentioned somebody named Swanson, and I've been thinking about that. Is there a possibility it could be the same man?"

Not unless Aunt Mellie lied, I thought. She'd lied before. Why? For the same reason as before, to punish me for snooping. "How can it be?" I said aloud. "You say he's a government surveyor, Aunt, that he's a horticulturist."

"How long ago was your Swanson at Montroth?"

"I don't know," I replied. "I gathered from what she said it was years. The greenhouse hasn't been used in a long, long time."

Stephen shook his head. "Well, you must be right. I'd have liked to take back some information, though, a shred of evidence that he's still alive, somewhere. Do you think we can have a look at the greenhouse? I just want to make doubly sure it's not the same Swanson."

"There's nothing," I said. "But I'll take you anyway."

His steps were just a bit more laggard, I thought, and I slowed my pace. We went around the house, and to the conservatory.

There was the one long aisle, the benches bare of activity, recent or otherwise. The same few earthen pots stood in the trays, but that was all.

Stephen had glanced up, his interest narrowing on the shelf loaded with jugs and jars of the clear liquid. "What's that?" When I explained he observed, "There's a lot of it."

"There is a lot of everything brought to Montroth, staples come in so seldom. Here," I said, and pointed, "is where I unearthed the wallet." I turned to find Stephen watching me intently, as if waiting for my next words.

"And—?" A small muscle twitched in his jaw.

I drew a deep breath; a sudden icy wind, like the exhalation from a grave, had touched my nerves. The initials on the wallet were *S.S.* Aunt Mellie could have been mistaken about the visitor's trade, and she had said Seivers. Leather would mold very rapidly, buried in the dirt. I'd not thought of it before. Yet what was the difference? Horticulturist or surveyor, the man had passed through here, and gone on his way. It was right and natural for Stephen to want information concerning a relative of an acquaintance. I'd have done the same myself. "It might have been the same person after all," I said slowly. "Aunt Mellie didn't actually say when he was here, I just assumed it was years ago because of the condition of the greenhouse. Where he went from here, though, I don't know, so I'm afraid it's not much help." Again I felt that icy cold, as when a door is opened and a draft blows through. I had to get out of here! "Shall we go?" I heard myself ask as from a great distance.

"This is a puzzle, but maybe I can still pick up his trail if there is one," Stephen said mildly as we moved back across the yard and to his quarters. At the door he turned. "Lori, I do thank you, and I hope you don't mind my free use of your given name. I've called you that so long in my thoughts, anyway."

"I—don't mind." I ached for him to kiss me, but he didn't.

"Will you be here tomorrow?"

I nodded, and left.

It was the first of the walks we were to take, but the tomorrow he mentioned didn't quite come about as planned.

I ate alone that night, at the great mahogany table with the candlelight glowing on silver and china and crystal. Bemused, I was not too hungry, but couldn't help appreciating the excellence of the meal—tiny rolls of beef with honey and mustard sauce, fresh peas and potatoes, blackberry wine.

I retired early, but found little sleep. I dreamed, and my dreams were all troubled ones, heavy with a sense of impending evil. I saw again the flickering light from the candles at the séance, and the shadows gathering beyond the reach of that feeble glow. Then the shadows became the gloom of the cellar, and the rush of wind, the squeaking of furry creatures around my ankles. I felt again that slow, enveloping horror which had no name, that was faceless. Slowly a figure began to emerge. It was Aunt Mellie peering through the strands of her grizzled hair, her eyes wide, maniacal, and burning like hot coals. I heard the swish of garments and saw her coming and tried to run but could not. I fell, crying out for help, but there was no one to come to my aid. I was alone.

The picture changed, and I was walking at the edge of the forest with Stephen, laughing and happy. Then the sun and blue sky were suddenly blotted out, and the air was heavy and thick. I looked for Stephen but he was gone. The darkness and shadows pressed down on me. I heard the sound of dry gasping breaths even as I woke and realized they were my own. My body was bathed in cold perspiration and the covering over me was wet and clammy with it. I sat up, clutching at the bedclothes. Something was wrong, very wrong!

I stumbled to my feet, staggered halfway across the floor, and doubled up with wrenching cramps. Somehow I made it to the bell-pull then back to bed, my teeth clenched against the waves of cramps and nausea.

It was still very early, sometime short of daylight, but the Jamaican woman came at once.

Hessit's fists flew to her mouth, and she burst into tears. I shook my head weakly. "It's all right," I gasped between paroxysms. "I'm all right." The excruciating pain was beginning to ease. "Just a little—give me a little while, I'll be fine. Maybe some cold—tea."

Hessit looked as though she were in shock. I repeated, "Cold, cold tea." I could sip it and I'd be fine. To be honest, I felt my stomach needed cooling. Hessit's eyes had flown wide. I repeated my wish a third time and she vanished on her errand. When she returned I was sitting up, having thrown off most of the cramps but still wrestling with the nausea.

Eyes and gestures asked a question. "It was the wine," I told her. "Pour out the wine, all that was in the decanter from which I drank at dinner. Wash the decanter thoroughly. Then dump all the wine—all the wine in the house, leave none of it. There has to be more poison somewhere. Search Aunt Lollie's rooms, Aunt Mellie's. All drawers downstairs. We haven't found it all. Wherever you have to go, whatever you have to do, *get it*."

The attack was swift, violent and short-lived. I'd been careless, drinking the wine. I'd been wrapped in my own thoughts, my own renewed hopes, and had forgotten it could be lethal. I'd seen Aunt Mellie stricken, Aunt Lollie made ill; knowing this I'd fallen victim to it myself through carelessness. Narcisse did not cook with wine, neither Aunt Lollie nor Aunt Mellie needed it, and the drink would no longer be a purveyor of poison in this house. The fact that I was young and strong had probably saved my life, that and the fact that I'd had only one small glass of the blackberry beverage—more would undoubtedly have meant the end of me. I knew this was a deliberate attempt upon my life. Hereafter I would eat in the kitchen.

Morning found me free of distress, subject only to brief intermittent weakness, and even this was wearing off. With only slight soreness in the abdominal region, I was able to stand on my feet and move about as before, and was very

grateful for my escape. Passing first Aunt Mellie's then Aunt
Lollie's doors, I noted all was tranquil, but at this moment I
found it difficult to care.

Aunt Lollie, who because of my defense of Stephen,
considered me too troublesome an interference and in their
way? Or Aunt Mellie, who undoubtedly knew Stephen had
not gone, and determined once and for all to put a finish
to what she believed had drawn him—me. Knowing how
she felt, I'd not confided in her, nor revealed his imminent
departure; I wouldn't give her that satisfaction.

The rubber plant in the hallway was dead, what once was
a large and healthy stalk with fine glossy leaves, collapsed
and fallen over the edges of the pot. So the wine that sweet,
helpful, and considerate little Aunt Lollie gave to speed her
injured sister's recovery, had been poisoned! And I was
supposed to be the carrier. I had all I could do to keep
from kicking the door open and challenging the old lady.
She hadn't cared how she accomplished her purpose. Only
that it was done. I felt my gorge rise in my throat as I turned
deliberately from both doors, and descended the stairs.

I had hot tea while Narcisse crashed about to the accompa-
niment of vituperative Cree French. She'd felt my forehead,
stubbornly insisted upon examining my tongue, and was all
for marching directly upstairs and having revenge. Hessit
of course had preceded me with the news.

Ana came up and stood soberly at my side. "For Lori,"
she murmured and placed the precious bracelet near my
saucer—an offering I knew had cost her.

I put my arm around her shoulders. "No," I said. "For
Ana. This is yours, keep it. I gave it to you, remember? For
you to keep. Here, let me put it back on again." This done, I
said, "There now. All yours," and sent her off with a pat.

Narcisse's eyes met mine. "That was a fine thing for her
to do," I said. "But don't you see? It's time to leave. She
doesn't have anyone to depend on, but you. I didn't know
this country very well when I came, but I've learned that
when it's this hot for this long, we're in for a storm. The

longer you wait the harder it will be to get out. If Jason and Haines have to stay, they can take care of themselves. But you take Ana and Hessit and *go*. Jason can get back before it breaks."

The big Indian woman wiped a brown arm across her sweating forehead. At ten in the morning the air was insufferably close. "Guess not. Many t'ing you do not know." Narcisse smiled pityingly. "Too much hurry. Run 'round in circles make big smoke, but not change anyt'ing. Lori fine girl but no see beyond end of nose. We *wait*, huh?"

"Wait," I said wearily, "wait for what?" I was trying to move a mountain. Frustrated, I looked up; Hessit stood in the doorway and she had a message. Aunt Lollie wanted to see me. I hesitated. So many times I'd dropped everything to run at these summonses! "She's not sick, is she? Not in need of anything?" Hessit shook her head. "Then tell her I'll come in a little while."

All too well I knew the pattern and wearily reviewed it. Aunt Lollie would be in a fit of pique over a slight, real or fancied, Aunt Mellie in a rage at some sly dig by Aunt Lollie, and the whole dangerous game would begin all over again.

I rose and followed Hessit out. Once, long ago, this Jamaican woman had warned me of danger, and I hadn't the slightest idea what she was talking about. Now I was asking her if all the liquor in the house was destroyed. She indicated that she'd located and disposed of a great store of the powders, and she was certain there were no more. What, I wondered, could they do to each other now?

Later I walked with Stephen, and his steps were firm, his carriage strong and upright. We spoke of commonplace things—the weather, which had become quite ominous, the clouds gathering thickly overhead.

How could I have fallen in love with someone I hardly knew? I'd seen compassion in him, and he could be gentle too. He was quick to rise against another's wrongs. We'd had moments of lightness and laughter, the humor he so admired in me more than matched by his own. But now I struggled to throw off a deep sense of sadness, of impending doom.

Again we moved around the house, down the driveway and back. Struck by a sudden raveling of pain I faltered, and Stephen quickly reached to steady me, then offered his arm. "Are you ill?"

"Just a bit of—I was, last night," I said, "but recovered rapidly. This, I am certain, is the last of it."

He had glanced back at the house, then stopped to study me narrowly. I could feel the sharpness of his gaze. "We can't be sure of that," he finally said. "We can walk another time."

"No, really," I protested. "I'm fine. You don't know how I look forward to getting out in the fresh air. Indoors can be confining. I'd rather continue, really I would."

"Well then, if you're sure."

He said nothing further. I looked up, and his face was set and grim. Was it concern for me? I took a deep breath, but the pain was all gone and I felt myself again. It had been only a fading remnant of the difficulty of the night before.

We went around the house, down the driveway and back. Stephen nodded toward the orchard. "Gnarled apple trees. I climbed trees like that when I was a youngster."

What could I say? I had no desire to take him to the orchard, or to go there myself. How could I tell him of the emanation that seemed to creep from it in the night hours, like something alive, to surround Montroth and all in it? How could I explain there was something in the greenhouse that sent cold chills down my spine, or that I felt a horror of the cellar as of something dead? Such words in the light of day would seem foolish. I couldn't admit to him that I was stricken with the same nonsensical superstition as Ana and Narcisse.

I was relieved when he asked, "Still all right?" I nodded and we moved on.

The tour took us, in part, to areas where we'd gone before. We came about by the dog pens and went up the path to the shrubbery bordering the small ancient garden. The tall grass was fully dry, and it was quite dark under the trees.

"A great little hideaway," Stephen remarked, walking forward. A pile of old boards stood in his way and he moved to step around it.

"Don't go there!" I cried out. "It might not hold you!" He was a big man, heavy, the last thing I wanted was for him to crash through the roof as I had done. "The cellar—remember the cellar? I said I'd fallen through it? The roof was rotten. It has since been repaired but I still didn't know—"

"That's the roof you went through?"

"Yes." I couldn't repress a shudder. "It was a chore getting out. It is dusty, full of barrels, old clothes and broken junk. And there were rats! If you don't mind, I'd as soon not talk about it any more. Are you ready? I'd like to get away from this place."

We walked for a short distance and he stopped, his arms opened. Without hesitation I went into them. I'd waited so long! His face slowly lowered to mine, and I was drowning in his kiss. His lips were heaven—sweet, tender, everything I'd ever hoped, then deeper, demanding, almost with desperation.

"Stephen—?"

"Yes." But his lips were claiming me, and what I would have asked was forgotten. His touch was fire, ecstasy. I couldn't think beyond the circle of his arms. My own arms were raised, my hands on his shoulders, my fingers clinging, caressing. I felt the lovely long length of his body pressed against me, as his mouth hungrily sought mine again.

I don't know how long we stood locked in each other's arms, murmuring words lovers have murmured since time began. He took my face gently in both of his big hands and touched my closed eyelids, then my lips, very, very tenderly. "Lori, I love you. I have always loved you—"

"And I, Stephen, I love you too. So much! Ever since that night—"

"That first night. I had to tell you that I love you. Whatever happens, remember I said it." He dropped his arms to his sides, looked at me a searching moment as if to impress my every feature on his mind, then swung on his heel and walked away.

What did he mean, whatever happened? I'd known he would go; he had to get back to his own job. Again I had a feeling of finality. I wanted to run after him, to beg him not to go, to ask why he hadn't given me that assurance that would have meant a future for us both. It was late in the day; he would spend the night in the lean-to. In the morning, would he be gone? I wouldn't even know when he left. I stood staring after him for a long moment then reminded myself of my duties. With dragging feet, I went inside.

Out of habit I checked first one, then the other, of my charges. Aunt Lollie was napping peacefully, Aunt Mellie sour and full of complaints.

"Going to storm and I suppose you're afraid. But it takes my sister—" she grimaced, "to blubber and carry on like an idiot. Where have you been? I told Hessit to fetch you but she was impudent—should discharge her. She has been acting odd of late, I cannot abide her any more. My word! When one could find proper help."

"Do you want anything?"

"No! Get out." The clawlike hand reached for a paperweight, and I backed away, closing the door firmly behind me. I'd been threatened with pokers, had books, dishes and jewel cases hurled at my head. There had been three attempts on my life, once with the flowerpot, once with the push down the stairs, then with poison. They had seesawed back and forth between themselves for years, how long before one of them devised a means other than poison and eliminated the other? Or me?

Somewhere I had heard the term incipient insanity. But this was progressive, the worsening noticeable even in the time I'd been here. The aunts had become more querulous, more tearful, more accusatory, and more violent. There were places to take care of people in this condition, and people trained to know what to do. Was I wrong in not seeking such help for the two little old ladies while there was still time? Or were they better off remaining here at Montroth, in the home they knew and loved, for what was left of their years?

I didn't go to bed that night but sat staring out the window trying to come to decisions best for all of us. When day broke at last, low and oppressive, I was scarcely aware of it.

Jason and Haines could flee farther into the forest and evade capture. They would be able to survive because they knew their way around the wilderness, at least Jason did and would help Haines. If they were careful, if they kept themselves back and out of sight and sound of others, they would be safe. It wouldn't be easy, but could be done.

I had coffee in the kitchen with Narcisse. "Where's Hessit?" I asked abruptly. "I haven't seen Hessit this morning."

Narcisse shrugged; she seemed singularly unconcerned and was moving briskly about her business. "Change beds. She do Missy M.'s now pretty quick. Always Missy M.'s first. That big job, you know."

I got up and prowled the room restlessly, then sat down again.

"What matter wit' breakfast?" The big Indian woman, arms akimbo, indicated the raisin bun growing cold in front of me. "Lori think too much, all time worry. Ever'thing be all right, be fine. See?"

I got through my second coffee, but pushed the saucer aside. "It's almost ten," I said at last, "I'll take Aunt Lollie's tray up to her if you'll fix it."

"Sure," Narcisse agreed cheerfully, "I fix." She turned suddenly and laid her brown hand gently on my shoulder.

"Ol' lady aunts take care of selves. No foolin'! See, Narcisse happy. Lori smile now, huh? For Narcisse."

Then I knew it was no use to protest, to strain and try to move things that would not be moved. "I'll take that tray now," I said, but at the doorway I turned. "Narcisse, you—you watch yourself and Ana real good today, will you? I have a feeling—"

"Only goin' storm," Narcisse chuckled, "good roof on house, Jason fix, Haines fix. Storm bad in these countree, summer, winter all same. Summer real bad, see many time. Bust things up dam' fine. All go boom—tree fall, hit othair tree, she fall. Lightning flash—what we care? Got plenty good food, coffee, tea, hotcake. Pret' soon storm go 'way. But Lori no know 'bout that? Brave girl, she all time brave, no be 'fraid of leetle storm. W'en you come back you stay here wit' me awhile. Narcisse make sads go 'way, you bet." Then seeing no smile, she added, "Aha. Leetle Owl-Eyes lon'some. No fine young mans. See heart go down road, cry inside. But maybe young mans come back, huh? Hurry up now carry tray, when come back, eat. Narcisse fix."

I couldn't rid myself of the dull ache. He'd loved me, and gone. He wanted no ties, no commitment, nothing to hold him back. He'd come to Montroth—not his choice—spent the time necessary, and gone on his way. I felt empty, lost.

I climbed the stairs slowly and rapped on Aunt Lollie's door. There was no answer, no movement inside that I could hear. Shifting the tray I knocked again, listening for the invitation that still didn't come. Alarmed, I tried the knob, and finding the door unlocked, entered.

Aunt Lollie was asleep, daintily curled on her side with one hand tucked under her withered cheek. Wisps of unbound hair had fallen over her face. I set the tray quietly on the table and approached the bed.

"Aunt Lollie," I said gently, "hot tea. Here, it's all ready for you." I touched her hand, then jumped back in horror. It was icy-cold, the hand of a dead person. A strand of hair slipped from her face to the pillow, and I saw that her eyes were wide open and staring, lips blue, flecked with foam and twisted into a grotesque gash.

I picked up the tray and walked out. At the foot of the stairs I met Hessit ascending with a load of linens in her arms. "Call Narcisse," I said. "Call Jason. Call everybody. Aunt Mellie has just killed her sister," and dropped the tray with a crash.

I went outside, needing to be alone. I walked to the lean-to; it was empty, Stephen gone as I'd known he would be. The sky was very dark; it might have been almost night. The big trees were still, waiting in the torrid atmosphere, and there was no sound anywhere, no bird-song, no birds soaring overhead. It was a dead world. The dogs were listless and lay quiet in the pen, heads on paws, tongues out and lolling. Haines had put out extra water for them, but I didn't see Haines now, and even Jason's axe was still. Then it came to me with a shock that Jason was waiting for me, Lori, to make the first move, that there was no one else to do it. Not Cook, not Hessit, not Haines. I turned and went back inside.

The house was a furnace, swollen with the fearful secrets it contained. Heat trapped between these walls gave off a rank, sulphurous odor; there was no breeze at all. I went upstairs and threw my windows wide, then methodically took off my dress to put on a cooler one. I sponged my face and arms in cold water; it was a momentary relief, but almost at once the stickiness returned.

It was afternoon now and a deep hush had fallen over the place. Ana huddled in the shadows, Narcisse puttered quietly around the kitchen. Fear was in her eyes at last. I'd managed to rally and take charge, with Jason to help. Aunt Lollie's room was shut and locked. Aunt Mellie, grinning evilly, had been locked into her own room. She was entirely insane. The poison she'd used in her final act had to be some she'd secreted, that Hessit in her diligence had failed to find.

I went downstairs and found Jason. With an ache in my throat I said, "I'm going for help. There has been one murder and will be more. We can't keep Aunt Mellie confined! Her quarters are not a jail; she has to be cared for properly. I would like you to drive me to the railway station. I'll let you off before we reach it, and I'll wait until you get away. Then I'll call for help. The station will have a telegraph. I know—you can't be here when help comes. There'll be many men, all strangers, and—" I choked. The old man was looking at me so kindly, so patiently. I plunged on. "You mustn't be here! Take Haines with you and go farther into the woods, as far as you can. They'll never find you there!" Tears spilled over and I wiped at them impatiently. I looked again at Jason standing so quietly before me and knew doubt. Hadn't he heard? He was smiling and calm. He wasn't going; he wouldn't leave!

"There's a settlement, Silver Springs," I cried desperately, still hoping to make him understand, "it's north of here so you can't go that direction." Thunder sounded softly around the rim of the world. Treetops beyond the clearing commenced to sway, lightly enjoined in a green-black ballet, and from afar came a soft moaning, a sigh which swept the skies, that mourned and wept as if the universe itself were in pain.

"Please! You *have* to go!" He was still smiling. Then he slowly shook his head. He made gestures, and pointed upward— one hour, less, and the storm would break. Coach and horses would not make it. They couldn't go.

I'd waited too long, and nobody would be driving anywhere. But I could walk! I didn't recall how far it was, probably not nearly as far as I'd thought, but what did it matter? I had all night. Aunt Mellie was secured, the mansion solid and strong; it could weather the storm as it had weathered storms in years past.

I ran for the house, and grabbed a little money, a scarf for my head, a coat, and a pair of stout shoes—the same ones I'd brought to Montroth with me so long ago. The house reeked of death, it was waiting, suspended in the breathless heat. Thunder grumbled again, louder now, and was almost immediately followed by the sharp, blue swish of lightning. It was close—too close?

Then I was out and running down the driveway, down the hill with the wind tearing at my coat, my scarf. Behind me the deep hush abruptly cracked wide open; thunder rushed and roared around the forest, then the very world was split by a mighty gash of lightning. The storm seemed centered in one place, as if Montroth were the target and all the elements conspired to aid in the assault.

My ankle turned sharply and I gasped. The odd, yellow glow in the atmosphere had given way to dull gray as the clouds sank lower, and suddenly, the rain came. It came first as a gentle patter, soft and fine, silken drops on my face, then harder, with a roar, pelting, almost a solid wall of water, and I was caught in it like a ship in the ocean.

I plunged on, half-blinded, and found my feet mired in the mud, my path blocked by rivulets of water trickling from the earth bank to my left and down across the road. Then as I watched, those small streams grew larger, fed by others from the cleared area below the orchard.

I realized with sinking heart that I'd not come as far as I thought. I hurried on, watching those streams in dismay, jumping over them when I could, wading through them when I could not. They were swiftly being joined by others and swelling into small raging torrents of dirty, brown water. In places they even now covered the road. With very little more pressure, the entire bank would give way, totally disintegrate. Already great canyons had been dug out of the rain-saturated earth, the force of the water carrying sticks and rocks and even a gnarled limb torn from an apple tree. I shuddered. Was that orchard fated to follow me even down here? It was like a curse.

I halted and brushed the wet from my eyes and looked back. Thunder reverberated, lightning slit the sky; wind whined in the treetops and branches bent into tortured

shapes beyond the mansion; I could barely see the huge
bulk of it, black through the sheets of driving rain. I gritted
my teeth and plunged on, drenched to the skin and shoes
oozing mud, but had gone only a few feet when I was
brought up short by a boiling, muddy torrent completely
blocking my path. There was no way past it and no way
to return—the bank, weakened by flood, by water washout
from above, was collapsing. It was a dam about to burst.
I screamed and jumped back, caught my foot on a rock
and fell. I looked up at the bank above me, then froze
in wordless horror—part of a man's hand and arm, with
the white of bones showing through and the tattered rags
of clothing still clinging to it, protruded from the soaked
earth. And there in the water and the mud and the remnants
of road, for the first time in my life, I fainted.

When I came to myself, I felt a rocking motion. I was
being carried by Jason. Rain plastered his grizzled hair to
his head; rain ran down his face and dripped off his chin.
We'd climbed partway up the hill and were on solid ground.
I stirred, and he stopped and set me down. Memory struck
me sharply, and I swayed and would have fallen had he not
put out a steadying hand. Blind horror choked me.

"The—the orchard—it flooded and I saw— The water,
it—*a man's hand came down in the mud*—!"

What I saw in his face stopped me. He knew? There was—
there had been a body buried in that orchard. Was this the
tortured spirit that roamed the place? Had Aunt Mellie—

I said it out loud, raising my voice above the roar of wind
and storm. "*Aunt Mellie?*" Jason nodded; his jaws worked
but no words came.

"I'm all right," I said, and with a mighty effort clamped
my teeth against the bile rising in my throat.

In unison, thunder roared and there was a sudden blinding
flash of jagged blue, a sharp hissing, then an explosion
which shook the earth. The very ground beneath me
trembled. The heavens were afire—the mansion had been
struck!

"Jason," I screamed, "go back to the house—see if they're all right! Hurry, hurry! I'll come—" Then I was stumbling up the hill. Jason was far ahead of me, already lost in the swirling storm.

By the time I reached the crest of the hill the whole north wing was ablaze. People were running about. I saw Hessit, Ana, and Narcisse. They'd gotten out safely and were huddled together in the rain. But where was Jason? He had completely disappeared; I couldn't see him anywhere.

So far the fire was confined to the north wing. From that quarter, smoke billowed and tongues of orange flame leaped high; through the swirling smoke a wild white-haired figure in a long flowing nightdress appeared on the upper balcony, screaming its thin scream and frantically waving its arms. Aunt Mellie! Why didn't somebody do something—get her down—help her? I leaped forward, but was driven back by a fierce blast of heat. Heat seared my cheeks and scorched my hair. Then I saw that someone else loomed on the balcony too, the squat form of Jason. He had calmly moved in front of Aunt Mellie and spread his great arms, holding her back. But the balcony was going to collapse, it would go down any minute!

I shouted until I was hoarse, unheard over the roar of the flames. Even as I watched, my blood turned to ice, a burning roof-timber plummeted earthward, momentarily blotting out the scene and narrowly missing them. Over the terrible roar of the fire I screamed at Jason to let Aunt Mellie go; they could get out—they could get out—

Down in the pen the dogs were crying wildly, and they suddenly exploded from their prison and ran every which way—Haines had turned them loose. The dog shelter erupted in a shower of sparks and smoke. The rest of the building had caught fire.

The balcony seemed to be held to the body of the house by the merest thread and when that let go—"*Jason!*" I screamed again and again started forward. "*Jason—*" He waved me back. The balcony shuddered, appeared to hang suspended for one long terrible moment, then plunged downward, part of the gable of the roof atop it, and was buried under tons of blazing debris.

I covered my eyes with my hands, weak and sick with shock and horror. I didn't feel the rain on my head, or know the wet on my cheeks was tears. Heat still pulsed from the house, flames still leaped, but the flashes of lightning were growing less, the wind dying down. The thunder moved on, grumbling, to the west. The fire was being beat down and put out, drowned by the downpour; even now only glowing embers smoldered in some places, small tongues of flame licking at the undersides of the timbers.

There wasn't any danger any more. The danger was past; only death remained. Jason was dead, buried somewhere beneath that simmering pyre. Aunt Mellie and Aunt Lollie too. It was as if the storm had come like some terrible avenging monster, had accomplished its purpose and moved on. The rain that fell now was as soft as a benediction.

Ana had ceased her whimpering, held close beside Narcisse. Hessit stood with an old coat over her head staring bewilderedly into the remains of the fire. She seemed unable to realize what had happened. I turned blindly at the sound of someone calling my name, and a tall figure loomed up out of the smoke and the rain and came toward me.

"Stephen?" Muddy, fire-streaked, and with no questions asked or answers given, I was enfolded in his embrace.

Epilogue

STEPHEN HAD NOT GONE as I had thought. He was at Montroth before I knew of it, before he became injured. Our encounter that night in Vancouver was no accident. He had not been far from me or from Montroth since my arrival, and Narcisse and Belinda had been taken into his confidence. Belinda left, realizing she could be no help to me if she remained, and might only be in the way.

Stephen was an undercover man investigating the disappearances—six, over the years—of travelers in the area. The most recent was Werner Venson, whose name I saw in the Vancouver newspaper. Barrels of formaldehyde in Montroth's cellar yielded clear evidence that the place was a trap. The body of Seivers, or Sigurd, Swanson, whose wallet I found, was there, and all those missing, save Venson, who had been buried in the orchard. How little I had known of the real activities of Montroth, its grisly traffic! When I allowed myself to dwell upon it, it still defied the imagination and sickened my soul. Poison was but a pastime, a trivial pursuit that kept two old ladies occupied. I had wondered, questioned, many times come near the truth, and in the end, narrowly escaped the same fate for myself.

It was Stephen of whom I'd caught a glimpse of as we left the train at Moose Station; Stephen who had gained entry to the mansion the night of the séance. He hadn't counted on broken ribs, which slowed his efforts, or falling in love, which complicated matters. He was in a most difficult position. This accounted for the distance I felt between us. Knowing what lay ahead, fearing for me, he had urged me to leave; I resisted, believing I was needed.

It was my mention of the cellar and its contents that gave Stephen the last vital piece of the puzzle. Before that day was out, he would have made his move, but the storm intervened.

It was as I had thought. The fall from her carriage had injured Aunt Lollie more than anyone believed, the accident bringing on mental deterioration. Aunt Mellie fled to Canada and seclusion as her sister worsened. Surrounding themselves with grateful but impaired servants added to their protection. Through the years, Aunt Mellie and Aunt Lollie learned to play the game of cat-and-mouse, and though hating each other, they made a team. There was no money, the aunts near-penniless squatters in the deep woods, the wills and the dusty documents in the tower room only worthless paper.

No wonder they resisted strangers! Knowing now what was buried in the orchard, hidden in the dark depths of the cellar I realized George was lucky to get away alive. Jason, I am sure, was responsible for the uninvited guest's safe departure.

Aunt Mellie and Jason died almost instantly. No trace was ever found of Aunt Mellie's or Aunt Lollie's bodies. Both were gone and their treasures with them.

Stephen had been on the other side of the house side trying to get in when the fire cut him off. Haines, after turning the dogs loose, was struck and killed by a falling timber.

It was guilt that incited Aunt Mellie's superstitious fear of the dogs, guilt that insisted the animals were ghouls, avenging spirits roaming the earth by night.

Long isolated at Montroth, Hessit and Ana and Narcisse were like frightened children. We—Stephen and I—have them here with us. I am round with child and a bit clumsy on my feet, it being the eighth month, and he insists I need help. Since it is my wish to bear many of Stephen's babies, undoubtedly the three will be with us always.

Our brutal memories of Montroth are fading; with the fall of the House its secrets are leveled forever. Grass has grown over the scars, the gentle forest has crept in, and this is the way we want to remember it. Shock and sorrow are past, and with Stephen at my side, I look forward to happiness and to peace.